WOVEN HEARTS

WOVEN HEARTS

•

Glen Ebisch

AVALON BOOKS
NEW YORK

PRINTED IN THE UNITED STATES OF AMERICA
ON ACID-FREE PAPER
BY HADDON CRAFTSMEN, BLOOMSBURG, PENNSYLVANIA

For My Mother

Chapter One

"We're doomed!" Rhonda announced.

Kate glanced up from the computer screen at her friend and business partner. As usual, Rhonda's flair for the dramatic was obvious. With her hands clutching the sides of the doorway into the shop and her arms outspread, the turquoise poncho that she'd probably gotten from Second Hand Rosie's up in Northhampton was spread out like the wings of an exotic bird.

"I see," Kate replied, turning back to the screen. "What is it this time? An asteroid coming to incinerate the planet, a seismic fault running through the northeast, or a newly discovered volcano in New England ready to erupt?"

Reading the tabloid headlines while waiting on the checkout line encouraged Rhonda's alarmist tendencies.

"Nothing like that. This is a serious disaster," Rhonda said, letting go of the door frame and stepping into Golden Needles, the quilt store that she and Kate co-owned.

As she came closer, Kate could see by the expression on her friend's face that she was genuinely worried.

"What's the matter?"

"Fabulous Fabrics," Rhonda said, naming a chain that was slowly spreading throughout New England selling cut-rate fabrics.

"What about them?"

Rhonda grabbed her chest like she was having a coronary. Her red-faced expression almost convinced Kate that she was.

"They're moving into the mall right up the road."

Kate felt a knot form in her stomach. Since she was the calm one, Kate knew she had to say something to Rhonda to ease her concern. But this, as Rhonda had said, was a serious disaster. Fabulous Fabrics not only had the buying power to undercut the prices of most small fabric and quilt stores, but they also had a huge inventory of lesser-quality goods that would easily fool an inexperienced sewer into thinking they were getting the same materials for less.

Golden Needles, which she and Rhonda had started two years ago, was just beginning to build a solid customer base and make a profit. All of that was now threatened by this new development.

"Are you sure?" Kate asked.

"Positive. I'd just left the supermarket and was driving past the big vacant store on the end. The door was

open and a man and woman were standing out front.
I stopped and asked them what was moving in there.
They said 'Fabulous Fabrics' clear as a bell. I couldn't
be mistaken."

"I see," Kate replied, feeling the knot in her stomach
tighten.

"What are we going to do?" Rhonda moaned, putting her head down on the counter. Her long red hair
hung down over her face like a veil. *Fortunately the
store is empty,* Kate thought. *A display like this
wouldn't help business.*

"One thing we are not going to do is panic," Kate
said with more firmness than she felt. "We don't know
whether a Fabulous Fabrics store will hurt us much or
not."

Rhonda peeked up at her and smiled hopefully.
"You really think it might be all right?"

Kate mustered a small smile of her own. Rhonda's
mood swings were like an express elevator that went
from the top floor to the basement without any stops
in between.

"No point in worrying about problems we don't
have yet. And one problem we do have is that you
promised to finish up those kits for the Log Cabin
class you're teaching tonight. Why don't you go back
in the workroom and get started on that? I'll look after
things out here."

Rhonda brightened. "I've got the fabric all picked
out. I'll get right on it."

*Thank goodness, Rhonda has something to do with
her hands,* Kate thought to herself as her friend went
into the back. The Log Cabin quilt design was a pop-

ular beginner project, and at least eight people had signed up for the class. It would take Rhonda all afternoon to get the kits ready. That would take her mind off Fabulous Fabrics. *Her mind, but not mine,* Kate thought grimly.

Although Kate was a highly skilled quilter as well, she handled mostly the business side of the shop, while Rhonda was the teacher. Despite her tendency to let her emotions run wild when it came to business matters, once Rhonda was in front of a class she was the picture of patience—not a quality that Kate had in large supply.

Kate turned back to the computer screen to check on their inventory. She tried to keep a close eye on which fabrics were selling and which ones were not. There were trends in quilts as in all areas of fashion, and a small store owner had to be sure she stocked what people wanted in ample supply, but she couldn't afford the mistake of buying bolts that wouldn't sell. Efficiency would be more important now than ever with a Goliath moving in right up the road.

The bell above the shop door rang. Kate looked up and was surprised to see a man in a business suit enter. He quickly disappeared down one of the aisles. Although one or two men belonged to her quilt guild which numbered over a hundred members, and there were a few nationally prominent male quilters, quilting was still primarily a female craft. Kate could go weeks at a time without seeing a man in the store.

"You should be selling sporting goods," her mother often told her, only half joking. "Then you'd find a replacement for Nick fast."

Nick, Kate thought. A picture flashed through her mind of dancing brown eyes and a comma of unruly black hair that always threatened to fall across his forehead. After almost a year together, on the very night she'd thought he was going to ask her to marry him, he'd announced that he was leaving the next morning for California to find himself.

"Find himself? I'd always thought there was something missing in the man," Kate's mother had said tersely. "Now at least we know what it was. There never was any Nick in Nick. The good Lord left the filling out of that candy."

Kate smiled to herself as she remembered her mother's comment. Her mother, who was still taking care of the small family farm in Vermont ten years after Kate's father had died. Her remarks could be blunt, but they were ususally right on target.

"Do you have this fabric in any other colors?" a man's voice asked. He cradled a bolt of fabric in his arms like a baby.

Kate looked up into the bluest eyes she'd ever seen. Like when the roller coaster reaches the top of its climb and pauses right before the gut-wrenching downward plunge, Kate's heart began to race with a combination of thrill and anticipation.

"Uh, no, I'm afraid we don't," she answered, breaking eye contact for a moment and sounding only slightly breathless.

"It is produced with a green and a black background as well as this blue, isn't it?" he asked with a smile.

She glanced at him again. He had light brown hair and a smile full of white teeth. His eyes seemed to laugh a little as he waited for her answer. Nice face, nice smile. Kate snapped her mind back to business and took a deep breath.

"Yes. It does come in three color schemes, but we only carry the blue. If you needed a lot of yardage of one of the others, I could special order it for you." *And I could deliver it to your home,* Kate said silently to herself.

"That's okay," he replied, looking into her eyes. "I was just wondering."

As he turned and walked back up the aisle, Kate watched him. He was tall, trim, and somewhere around thirty, she guessed, with no wedding ring on the left hand.

Kate forced her attention back to the computer screen, but all the words seemed to have run together and the rows of numbers made no more sense than a top-secret code.

"When you see something you want you've got to go right at it. It's not going to trip over you without some help," Kate could hear her mother saying.

"But what if he's another candy without a filling?" Kate asked out loud.

"Excuse me. Did you say something?"

Kate jumped. The man had returned to the counter. She'd been too preoccupied to hear.

"Just talking to myself. An occupational hazard when you work alone."

"Do you run this shop by yourself?"

"I have a partner. She's in the back right now, but we usually take shifts working in the store."

The man nodded. "I see. Well, you have a very nice selection of fabric here."

"I'm Kate Manning," she said, sticking her hand across the counter. She did it so quickly it looked like a karate chop, but at least her mother couldn't say she hadn't tried.

The man hesitated, then took her hand. "I'm Roger Garrison," he said.

Kate felt the warmth of his touch travel up her arm. She hoped her thumb didn't feel too coarse from all the times she'd stuck it with the needle while quilting. She let her mind focus on where his hand touched hers. Did he seem a bit sorry when he finally let go? Kate wasn't certain, but she thought so.

"Are you a quilter yourself?" Kate asked. *Or are you looking for your wife or girlfriend? Hopefully, your mother?* she thought.

"Actually—"

Before he could answer, the bell over the door rang shrilly as a woman wearing a dark green business suit walked in. Kate recognized the outfit as being one of the recent styles she'd seen in the pattern books. But it was unlikely this woman had made it herself. Everything from her carefully ruffled hair style and perfect makeup to her long polished nails and high heeled shoes said that she bought whatever she wanted. Very tall and slender, about a size six, Kate thought.

"Roger, I'm done," she announced impatiently, waving a cell phone in his direction.

Roger frowned. "Kate, this is Melissa Hardgrove. Melissa, this is Kate Manning."

Melissa nodded in Kate's general direction, at the

same time rolling her eyes as if to indicate that one of Roger's charming eccentricities was introducing her to unimportant people.

"I was just telling Kate what a fine selection of fabrics she has in her shop."

Melissa swiveled her head quickly. "The shop is rather quaint."

For an instant Kate could see the store through the woman's eyes. A small corner shop at the end of a not very elegant strip mall. Two sides of windows saved it from being claustrophobic, but it wasn't much larger than the first floor of a small house; three aisles of fabric, a few racks of supplies, and the rest of the store area given over to tables for classes. For one blinding moment, it seemed to Kate, who was usually so proud of what she had accomplished, that Golden Needles was really rather pathetic. Maybe it was time for Rhonda and her to admit that the whole idea of having their own store was like little girls playing house. Just two young women who hadn't really grown up pretending they could run a business.

Kate could also see herself standing there in jeans and a sweat shirt that said "Quilters Keep It Together." Her chestnut brown hair could use a trim, and she couldn't remember the last time she'd bothered with makeup. Although Kate knew most people would describe her as petite with a nicely rounded figure, she felt frumpy and forelorn across from the fashion model perfect Melissa in her power suit.

Melissa tapped the gold watch on her wrist and gave Roger a meaningful look. He opened his mouth to speak when Kate heard a shriek behind her.

She turned and saw Rhonda standing in the opening to the back room. Rhonda had one arm outstretched, her poncho thrown back over her shoulder. Her finger was pointing directly at Roger as if she were about to shoot him in a duel.

"He's the man," Rhonda shouted accusingly.

Roger gave her a puzzled look.

"What are you talking about?" Kate asked calmly, hoping some of it would rub off on Rhonda.

"He's the man from Fabulous Fabrics."

No one spoke for a moment.

"Is that true?" Kate asked, staring deep into Roger's eyes and feeling betrayed.

"I was about to tell you when Melissa came in. Honestly, I was."

"You don't have to apologize to her," Melissa said. A small smile crossed her face. "There's not even any reason to get to know her. Once our store is up and running, she won't be around long anyway."

"That's enough, Melissa," Roger snapped.

Anger flashed across her perfect face, then she shrugged. "These people are nothing. If you want to talk to people who are nothing, I'm going to wait in the car."

With a toss of her shiny black hair, she turned and walked away. Her heels clicked like castanets on the tile floor as she left.

Roger's eyes never left Kate. "I was going to tell you. You have to believe that."

"Spy!" Rhonda hissed.

Kate looked back at her friend. "Okay, Rhonda, that kind of talk won't help. Don't forget those kits."

Giving Roger a last fierce glance, Rhonda disappeared into the back room.

"I'm not a spy," Roger said. "I just came in to see what your store was like."

"Sounds like scoping out the competition to me," Kate replied.

Roger smiled guiltily. "Okay, maybe that was part of the reason I came in here in the first place. But I really like your shop, and I enjoyed talking to you. I know this is kind of awkward under the circumstances, but I was hoping that maybe we could continue our conversation over dinner."

His eyes locked on Kate's again, and she felt her heart quiver. But she was determined that feelings weren't going to stop her from saving her business.

"That's a nice idea. But it seems to me that no matter how well we get along, your store is going to make things pretty hard for us. Like that fabric you asked about, I bet you'll carry it in all three colors and sell it cheaper than I can. Isn't that right?"

"Yes, that's probably true," Roger admitted. "But that's business, Kate. I can't do anything about it. Does that have to stop us from being friendly competitors?"

"Friendly enemies is more like it."

"I'd never want to be your enemy, friendly or otherwise."

"And what about Ms. Perfect?" Kate asked, nodding toward the parking lot. "Is she part of business too?"

"She's my assistant. It's nothing more than business."

For a moment Kate saw his eyes shift away from

hers. She knew there was more to it than he was letting on.

"Since we're going to be competitors," Kate said, "then maybe we'd better make it nothing more than business between us too, then."

She pressed her lips together firmly so they wouldn't quiver, and so she wouldn't say something that might sound weak.

"I'm sorry to hear that," Roger said, anger and sadness seemingly mixed in his voice. He turned and walked out the door.

"You were pretty hard on him," Rhonda announced from behind her.

Kate turned and gaped at he friend. "You were the one who pointed at him like he was a convicted felon."

Rhonda grinned. "Yeah. But he is kind of cute."

Chapter Two

A week later, Kate was at a quilt show in southern Vermont. She, along with the representatives of a number of other quilt stores, rented space there every year to sell fabics and supplies to the people who attended the show. The doors had just opened and Kate was standing behind a table piled high with bolts of cloth. She was thinking about how beautiful it was to drive out through the Berkshires to southern Vermont in October when the leaves still covered the trees in brilliant colors. Getting out of the shop this time of the year was a pleasure.

Sometimes Kate felt that life was passing her by while she sat behind the counter at Golden Needles. The shop was open six and a half days a week, and even though she and Rhonda tried to divide up the time, many days they had to be there together when there were classes to teach or paperwork had to be done. And shows like this one, however enjoyable, tied up an entire weekend. They had discussed hiring a part-time employee so they could get a few more hours for themselves, but they couldn't pay much and still keep within their budget.

Oh, well, Kate thought, those are the sacrifices that come with owning your own business. The benefits are not having a boss telling you what to do and getting pleasure out of seeing the store become successful.

"Hello again."

Kate jumped. Roger Garrison stood in front of her. A small smile played across his lips and his blue eyes seemed amused.

"Sorry if I startled you," he said.

Kate grunted disbelievingly. Thinking about making a success of Golden Needles, then seeing the likely cause of its failure sent her spirits plummeting.

"Do you think I go around purposely frightening women?"

"I wouldn't be surprised." Kate knew she was being unfair, but this was a man she had to keep at a distance.

"Whoa," Roger said, putting his hands out in front of him. "Can't we start over again?"

"Are you still the manager of the soon-to-be-opened Fabulous Fabrics store right up the road from me?" Kate asked.

"Sure."

"Then I don't see how there can be any new starts. You're going to do your best to put me out of business, and I'm going to do whatever I can to stop you. The best we can be is worthy adversaries."

Roger laughed. "This is starting to sound like some kind of kung fu movie. Are you staying over in town tonight?"

Kate fumbled with some items on the table in front of her so she wouldn't have to look him in the face. Whenever she looked at him she wanted to say nice things, to laugh and joke and ask him to take her out on a date. She could hear herself now telling people that she was being put out of business, and when people asked by whom, she could say like an idiot, "By my boyfriend, of course."

"Yes. I'm staying over," she answered, trying to keep her tone businesslike if not frigid.

"At the Overlook Hotel?"

Reluctantly Kate nodded. Most of the sellers at the show stayed there because they got a special rate.

"How about dinner tonight, then? No talk about business, I promise. I'm sure that we've both got enough things happening in our lives that our conversation doesn't have to focus on fabric."

She made the mistake of glancing up into his blue eyes which at the moment seemed so sincere that she almost accepted his offer.

"One of the strangest things about life," her mother often said, "is that you either can't get what you want or, when it comes along, you don't want it anymore."

Here was a man she would have gone out with like a shot under normal circumstances, and now, when he was almost throwing himself at her, Kate found that she really didn't want to let herself get involved, not with a competitor.

"I'm sorry," she said firmly. "But I'm having dinner with one of my friends from another shop. Thanks for asking me."

Roger shrugged and smiled. "Okay. But I'm not going to give up, you know."

"Give me a call if you ever go into another line of work," Kate said. She meant her remark to sound light and flippant, but it came out as a serious offer.

"If only I could," Roger replied somberly. Giving Kate a small wave, he wandered off up the aisle.

The show was a busy one. Staffing the space alone, Kate was worked off her feet until about a half hour before the show was due to close for the day. Even though tired, she smiled to herself as she counted the receipts. A show like this could bring in more money in two days than a month at the shop. If she'd dared to close the shop for an entire weekend, she and Rhonda together could have made even more money. A number of people had left her booth because the lines were too long.

As she was getting ready to leave, Kate remembered that she had told Roger she was going to have dinner with a friend. Not wanting to be a liar, she went over to the table for the shop where her friend Monica worked. Monica was a few years older than Kate. She and her partner had a thriving store in the Albany area. Dinner would be a good chance to pick Monica's brain about the sorts of things she might do to survive the Fabulous Fabrics attack. Maybe they could go somewhere after dinner so it wouldn't seem like such a long lonely night.

"Hey, Monica, are you free for dinner?" Kate asked.

Monica looked up from a box of material she was bending over.

"Sure, Kate, but it'll have to be at the Overlook's dining room and on the early side. How about around six? I'm going out to a movie with some folks later on."

"Fine."

But that only took care of dinner. *Long lonely night here I come,* she thought to herself glumly.

A few minutes before five-thirty Kate took a seat at a table in the restaurant. The hotel was crowded and even at this early hour the tables were starting to fill up. She was so busy craning her neck to spot Monica as she walked into the restaurant that Kate didn't notice the man until he slid into the booth across from her.

"Hello, little honey," he said grinning at her and blinking rapidly as if his eyes had trouble focusing.

From the reek of alchohol traveling across the table in her direction, Kate was surprised that he could see at all. He'd probably come in through the door from the bar.

"You don't really want to have dinner in this place, do you? Let me take you some place where we can have a really good time."

"I'm waiting for a friend. He's going to be here shortly."

The man laughed his disbelief. "Why don't we wait for him together?"

Kate wasn't really afraid. She was in a busy public place, and Monica would be along soon. But spending any more time than she had to across from this drunk was more than she could stand.

"How about you wait by yourself," Kate said, starting to rise.

Quicker than she'd have thought him capable of doing in his condition, he grabbed her wrist.

"No woman walks out on me," he said, suddenly sounding more angry than drunk.

Kate dropped back in the seat. She was getting ready to shout and create a scene when she became aware of someone else standing by the table.

"Is this my replacement?" Roger asked. "I thought you had better taste."

"Get lost, buddy," the drunk muttered. "The lady's with me now."

Roger leaned over the table and put a hand on the man's shoulder. Kate saw him flinch as Roger tightened his grip.

"How about you go back to whatever bar you wandered in from?" Roger said in a still friendly voice.

The man slowly got to his feet. For a long moment he looked at Roger who was about a foot taller and ten years younger than he was. Roger kept his eyes fixed on the man. Finally the moment passed.

The man turned and waved a hand as if chasing flies. "Yeah, whatever. It's not worth the trouble," he said as he walked with excessive care back in the direction of the bar.

Roger stood watching the man until he left the room, then he slid into the seat across from Kate.

Kate found she'd been holding her breath. She exhaled deeply.

"Thanks," Kate said, surprised at how relieved she felt. She must have been more frightened than she realized.

Roger reached across the table and took her hand. Too startled to move, she watched while he pressed her hand gently to his lips.

"Your humble servant, ma'am." He looked up at her, his eyes dancing wildly.

She pulled back her hand. "I'll bet you say that to all the girls."

"Only the ones who keeping turning me down for a date."

"Quite a crowd, is it?"

Roger laughed. It was a deep infectious laugh, and Kate found herself joining in. *A man who can laugh at himself,* she thought, *well that is a rarity.*

"But I really can't say that I think much of your lying to me to get out of dinner. That doesn't do much for a man's ego."

"I didn't lie," Kate said a bit huffily. "I am meeting a friend for dinner."

"I'll bet you had imaginary friends as a child too." Roger's eyes sparkled with mischief. "Is your friend sitting here right now? Maybe you'd like to introduce us." He pretended to glance under the table and to peek behind the vase of artificial flowers.

Kate suppressed a smile and looked up at the hostess station. She didn't see Monica yet but instead saw Melissa Hardgrove. Tonight she was wearing a blood red dress with a full skirt that swirled gracefully around her slim legs which were moving rapidly in Kate's direction. From the expression on her face, Kate was relieved for the second time that night that she was in a public place.

"I don't think it's any imaginary friend that you have to worry about right now," Kate said.

Roger looked at her, puzzled.

"I was waiting for you in the lobby," Melissa said, standing over Roger. The tone of her voice clearly implied that waiting for him was an activity she'd never experienced before and didn't intend to ever experience again.

Roger looked more uncomfortable than he had when facing down the drunk.

Kate felt an overwhelming desire to puncture the woman's veneer.

"Roger and I were just trying to decide whether to have dinner together," Kate said, smiling sweetly.

Melissa looked down her nose at Kate. "You must have misunderstood. Roger and I are going out to dinner."

"Did I misunderstand you, Roger?" Kate said, looking as innocent as possible.

"Well, I . . . uh . . . when you said you were having dinner with a friend, I invited Melissa."

"My fault then. I guess you're right, Melissa, you are the second choice," Kate said, smiling up at the woman, who turned visibly red even under her perfect tan. "Well, run along, you two, and have a wonderful time. I see my friend coming now."

Roger shook his head with a mixture of sympathy and pity at Kate's continued fabrication of dinner with a friend. He stood up, took Melissa firmly by the arm, and began leading her away. She resisted for a moment, primed to continue her conversation with Kate, but finally she seemed content with giving Kate a contemptuous look and allowed herself to be led away.

"Hi," Monica said as she arrived at the table a second later. She looked quizzically at the couple that had just walked past her. Roger glanced back. He saw Monica and his eyes widened in surprise. Kate winked.

"What was that all about?" asked Monica.

"Just a guy who thought that he might want to have dinner with me. I told him I had an appointment with a friend, but he wouldn't believe me."

Monica rolled her eyes. "I appreciate that we're friends and all, but if a guy like that asked me out to dinner, I'm afraid that you'd come in a distant second. Why'd you stand him up?"

"Well, he had a replacement in reserve, as you can see."

"The model who was looking at you like you'd just run over her pet Chihuahua?"

"That's the one."

"You aren't telling me that was your only reason for turning him down. A guy like that will always have women hanging around him."

Kate sighed. "He's also my worst enemy."

"Well, honey," Monica said with a grin, "if you think he's the enemy, you must be fighting the wrong war."

Chapter Three

Kate stood behind her table at the quilt show the next morning and felt guilty. She had tossed and turned the night before, filled with remorse for what she had done. Just because she wanted to taunt Melissa, she had put Roger on the spot by revealing to an obviously jealous and possessive Melissa that Roger had invited her out to dinner. Instead of being nice to him after he'd saved her from an obnoxious drunk, she'd gotten him into trouble.

"You've got a sharp wit, Kate," her mother would often say. "That's a good thing, but like anything sharp, you've got to be careful how you use it."

I should have been nicer, Kate admitted to herself, but why was Roger asking me out when he clearly has some kind of relationship going with Melissa? Roger claimed that she was only his assistant, but she acts more like his girlfriend or even his fiancée.

Whatever the truth, Kate concluded, Roger seemed like a guy who could end up being trouble. Lots of good-looking guys were. *Haven't I learned anything from my year with Nick?* she asked herself. All her friends had said he was a doll. That was the problem, he was a doll, not a man.

Kate bent down to pick up a large box filled with heavy bolts of cloth. Her hands couldn't quite get a grip. It was starting to slide out of her grasp when another pair of hands seized the box and held it steady.

"Good morning," Roger said. "Where would you like this?"

Kate pointed to the table.

He was wearing a blue sweater that accentuated the color of his eyes. As he placed the box where she had indicated, Kate noticed he was wearing a pair of jeans that showed he was in good shape. She quickly took her eyes away from his body as he turned back to smile at her.

"So there really was a friend you were going to have dinner with last night," Roger said. "You had me fooled."

"I don't lie," Kate said, sounding so prim that she could have kicked herself.

"When you're in the bulk fabric business long enough, you start to forget that some people are honest."

"Have you been with Fabulous Fabrics long?"

He shook his head. "Only a couple of years. Before that I worked for a big fabric manufacturer in the design department. That's how I met the owner of Fabulous Fabrics. He was on a tour of our plant, and we started talking about new fabric designs."

"Is this your first time as a store manager?"

"Actually, I'm only the temporary manager. I open stores and manage them for six months or a year until they start making a profit. Then I move on to the next one. This will be my third."

"You mean you stay there just long enough to drive out the small quilt shops that might compete with you," Kate tried to smile as she spoke, but by the expression on Roger's face she could tell the words had stung. She raised a hand in a gesture of peace. "Sorry, that was out of line."

He smiled faintly. "What you said isn't far from the truth but isn't it the same in any business? The big stores drive out the little ones unless they can find a special niche."

Kate shrugged. "Why did you come to this show? Fabulous Fabrics isn't planning to start doing quilt shows now too, are they?" That would really be the frosting on the cake, to have to compete with the giants even at the quilt shows.

"No," Roger said. "Even if we wanted to, the quilt shows wouldn't have us. They favor the small shops. I'm just here out of a personal interest in seeing what's new in fabric design this year. Like I said, that's what really got me into the business in the first place."

"And is the Dragon Woman interested in fabric design as well?"

Roger looked bewildered for a moment, then he laughed. "Oh, you mean Melissa. She can come on a little strong sometimes, but that's because Melissa thinks she always has to prove what a tough businesswoman she is."

There's more to it than business, Kate wanted to say. *Unless you included monkey business.* She wanted to ask him again exactly what his relationship to Melissa was, but somehow that seemed kind of personal. It also would suggest that it mattered to her, and Kate wasn't about to get involved with her toughest competitor no matter how nice he was.

Maybe that was why he was such a good store opener? He went around and sweet-talked all the female shop owners so they didn't know what was happening until the day came when they couldn't meet the rent. Kate spotted Melissa standing at the end of the aisle. She was scanning the crowd, and Kate figured she knew the person Melissa was trying to find.

"Speak of the devil," Kate muttered.

Roger followed the direction of her glance and sighed.

"Before we get interrupted, I want to say thank you for helping me out last night. I appreciate it," Kate said.

"Did it prove that I'm a guy you'd let take you to dinner?" he asked.

He reached over and touched her hand. She felt the warmth travel up her arm. Without consciously wanting to, she put her other hand over his.

"I'd really like to, Roger." She saw his face light up. "But the way things are I really don't think that would be a good idea."

"You mean because we're competitors. I told you we could be friendly competitors."

"It's that . . . and other things." *Such as the one heading this way right now,* Kate thought.

Melissa had spotted them and was moving like a locomotive down the crowded aisle, casually elbowing people out of the way. She was wearing violet today, Kate noted, but there was certainly nothing shrinking about her.

"You'd better head Melissa off at the pass," Kate warned. "She looks like she's in the mood to create a scene."

Roger turned and let go of Kate's hand. He rushed up the aisle and caught Melissa while she was still several yards away. Melissa clearly wanted to have it out with Kate, but Roger took her arm and gently guided her in the opposite direction.

"That woman's got it bad," Kate said out loud to no one in particular. Just then her cell phone rang.

"Hello," Kate answered.

"This is Rhonda. I've got a big problem."

Since Rhonda had been left alone in charge of the store, Kate immediately pictured a fire roaring through their highly flammable inventory or a broken water main turning the store into a pool filled with bobbing bolts of expensive fabric. Then reason set in and Kate figured it might just be that Rhonda's highly erratic blow dryer was on the fritz again. Who could tell?

"What is it Rhonda?" Kate asked calmly.

"Mom!"

"Whose mother?" Kate felt her heart sink.

"Mine. Who else?"

Kate refrained from mentioning that she too had a mother.

"What about your mother?"

"She broke her leg."

"I'm sorry to hear that," Kate said. "How did it happen?"

"She tripped over the rug in the hall."

Kate wasn't surprised. She'd met Rhonda's mother once, a middle-aged version of Rhonda who was also inclined to leap before she looked. Rhonda's mother had lived by herself in California for as long as Kate and Rhonda had been friends. Rhonda's father died many years ago, and her mother worked in some branch of the state government.

"I have to go take care of her. It's her right leg, so she can't drive, and somebody has to do the shopping and stuff."

Kate took a deep breath. Running the store with two people was hard enough; how was she going to manage by herself?

"Couldn't somebody else in your family do it?"

"You know my brothers live in the midwest, and they've got regular jobs. They can't just take off."

And you can? Kate wanted to say. One of the problems with being in a partnership with Rhonda was that she thought owning your own business meant that you didn't have to keep regular hours or worry about having a set routine. What that usually came down to was Kate filling in while Rhonda did something she just couldn't say no to.

"When are you leaving?" Kate asked, resigned to the inevitable.

"Right now. That's why I called. I put a closed sign in the store window. Karla is going to pick me up in fifteen minutes and take me to the airport."

Couldn't you have at least waited until tomorrow to

leave and kept the store open today? Kate wanted to say, but she realized that there was no point in getting into an argument with her obviously distressed friend. Since she and Rhonda also shared an apartment on the second floor of a two-family house, not only was she losing help in the store, but she would also probably end up paying the entire month's rent on her own.

"How long will you be gone?" Kate asked.

"Don't know. Six weeks, maybe more. Mom isn't as young as she used to be."

She's only fifty, not a hundred and five, Kate thought and bit her tongue.

"Well, good luck and give your Mom my best."

"So long."

The phone went dead. *If I'm lucky,* Kate said silently to herself, *her mother will be glad to get Rhonda out from underfoot inside a month.*

They say trouble comes in threes, Kate thought as she hurried to wait on a customer. *Well, I've got Fabulous Fabrics breathing down my neck, and now my partner decides to take off for California. I wonder what the third thing will be.*

Another busy and profitable day for Golden Needles was over. Kate smiled with satisfaction as she wheeled the hand truck piled high with boxes out to her car. Between customers, she'd managed to put things in perspective. If the craft shows continued to do well, the store might possibly survive the onslaught of competition from Fabulous Fabrics. She had a solid customer base, and although Rhonda's absence would force her to cancel some of the scheduled quilting classes, Kate could take on a few of them herself. Maybe she'd run an ad in the paper for a part-time employee. She couldn't afford to pay more than the minimum wage, but possibly she'd find a person who would be willing to take the job for an employee discount on fabric.

Kate opened the side door of her van. She put the first box inside the cargo area and climbed inside the van to push it into the farthest corner. There was a crash behind her. Kate scrambled backwards and saw that the hand cart had toppled over on its side. Several boxes had opened, spilling fabric onto the asphalt.

"Oops! It looks like something fell over."

Kate stared at Melissa, who was standing there with a falsely sweet smile.

"Sorry. I guess I just didn't see your little wagon there."

Kate felt a flash of anger and wanted to wipe that smug smile off Melissa's face. Then the image flashed before her of two women fighting in the parking lot outside a quilt show. She chuckled to herself; that would certainly create a sensation.

Ignoring Melissa, Kate bent over and began to re-pack. When she was done, she picked up a box and turned to shove it into the van. Melissa blocked her way.

"I'm warning you, stay away from Roger."

The intensity in Melissa's voice made Kate pause. Then she moved toward Melissa, using the box as a battering ram. Melissa quickly jumped out of the way, not wanting to get her violet outfit soiled. Kate tossed the box into the van and turned back to face the other woman. Wearing her usual high heels, Melissa towered over her by a good four inches, so Kate had to look up into the other woman's angry face.

Kate put her hand on her hips. "Look, I'm tired of putting up with your childishness. I've got a store to run, and now with my partner away I have a lot to do without dealing with your irrational jealousy. I am not chasing Roger, and if you're having so much trouble hanging on to him, maybe you'd better ask yourself what's wrong with you, rather than spending your time threatening me."

Melissa's eyes narrowed, and she reached forward with one of her sharp pointed fingernails to poke Kate in the chest.

"Just remember, you've been warned. I get what I want, and once I have it, nobody takes it away from me."

Not waiting for an answer, Melissa turned and quickly walked over to a red sports car. Giving Kate one last malevolent look, she slipped behind the wheel. Revving the engine and kicking up gravel in Kate's direction, she sped out of the parking lot.

Swell, Kate thought to herself, *I've been doing everything I can to avoid the guy, and now I've got his witchy girlfriend threatening me. Well, at least that was the third bad thing. Maybe I'll have smooth sailing for a while.*

Kate picked up another box and the bottom fell out.

Chapter Four

This can't go on, Kate mumbled to herself. She heard the coffee dripping into the pot in the workroom. That was about the only thing keeping her awake these days. Ten o'clock in the morning and already it felt like it was ten at night. On top of running the store all day, she'd taught a quilting class that lasted until nine-thirty the night before. That was the third evening class she'd taught in the last week. The ten days since Rhonda had left blurred into one long day at the shop. She staggered home at night too tired to cook, grabbed whatever she could find from the refrigerator, then tumbled exhausted into bed.

If only someone would answer her ad for a part-time employee. It had been running for almost a week in the Hampden County Record. A number of people had called, but most had lost interest when Kate told them the pay. Three had gotten as far as coming in to

31

see her. They hadn't seemed discouraged by the money, but their obvious lack of any knowledge about fabrics was a problem. Training someone to cut material and to help customers match colors and patterns would take as much, if not more, effort than running the shop herself. The person would just be getting up to speed in time for Rhonda to return.

Kate was in the back room pouring coffee into a mug with a smiley face on it when the bell rang. She glared at the grinning mug and swore that she was going to throw it away even though it belonged to Rhonda. When she got to the counter, a woman of about twenty stood there with an even bigger smile than the one on the mug.

"Hi, I'm here about the job," she said eagerly. "My name is Sandra Lester."

She thrust her hand over the counter. Kate blinked to clear her head, then took Sandra's hand, wondering if this level of enthusiasm was natural.

Kate explained the job and told her the pay. Surprisingly, Sandra still seemed pleased. She was especially excited at the prospect of getting a discount on her fabric purchases.

"You've got really lovely things here," she said, letting her eyes travel around the shop. "I do a lot of quilting and make some of my own clothes. Getting discounts on great material is just what I need."

"Do you have any experience working in a quilt store?" Kate asked. She feared the worst. This person was definitely too good to be true.

"Oh, sure. I used to work in a quilt store back home."

"Where is that?"

Sandra waved behind her. "Back near Boston."

"What brings you out here?" Kate asked.

"I'm going to college," she said and named a local school.

"Will you be able to put in twenty hours a week and still go to class?"

"No problem if my hours are in the afternoon and evening. And I can really use the money. School is awfully expensive."

Not being able to think of any more questions, Kate told Sandra she could have the job for a two-week trial to make sure they were both happy with the arrangement. They agreed that she would start tomorrow afternoon.

"You won't regret this," Sandra said, seizing Kate's hand again.

As Sandra gave her a big wave good-bye from the door, Kate wondered if adjusting to all this enthusiasm was going to be even more tiring than doing all the work herself.

Was I ever that thrilled with life? Kate asked herself. True, now she was seven years older than Sandra, but even when she'd been in college, Kate would never have called herself bubbly. Maybe it was because of her father dying when she was sixteen, but her mother had told her that even as a young child she'd been kind of serious.

In college Kate had taken some art courses, which she had loved, but eventually she majored in business because that was the sensible path to a good job. About the most spontaneous thing she'd ever done,

Kate knew, was to give up her good position at the insurance company after four years and buy Golden Needles. Steady promotions and good benefits—the company had dangled them before her, trying to dissuade her from leaving. Kate would admit that she'd been tempted, but somehow the idea of pulling into the same giant parking lot and walking into the same huge building to do pretty much the same job day after day depressed her.

She had always saved much of what she earned, not quite sure why, but instinctively Kate knew that some day an opportunity would come along and she wanted to be ready for it. Then Kate had run into Rhonda, an old friend from college, and the dream of Golden Needles had been born. Rhonda had borrowed some money from her family, and combined with much of Kate's savings, it had been enough to launch the business.

Kate had worried the whole night before telling her mother of her plan. She fully expected that, as a practical farm woman, her mother would shake her head sadly and say it was absolute idiocy to ever give up a well-paying job.

Her mother had surprised her.

"Working for yourself is never easy because you can't be sure of things from one year to the next. But at least you get to take credit for all your successes and that doesn't usually happen when you work for a lot of other people." Then her mother had smiled. "Of course, you also get to take the blame for your mistakes."

Kate sighed. There had been some of both so far.

Her mind drifted back to Roger. Even though she hadn't seen him since the quilt show, he still appeared in her thoughts every day. She'd catch herself sitting dreamily in front of the computer screen remembering his glance, his touch, the way he smiled. She would hear the bell over the shop door ring and look up with a big silly smile on her face expecting it to be him.

Had turning down his invitation to dinner been one of her successes or one of her biggest mistakes? Maybe now with Sandra taking over some of the work, she'd have a chance to rest and think. Although Kate wasn't sure that thinking would help. Too bad she couldn't be like Rhonda who felt and then acted without the inconvenience of including her brain in the process. Sometimes that made Kate furious with her partner, but other times she envied her friend's youthful spontaneity.

The bell over the door rang and Kate looked up happily, expecting to see Roger come into the shop. Instead, one of her regular senior citizen customers appeared in the doorway. *I've got to stop acting like a teenager with a crush,* Kate warned herself.

"Hi, Lucy," Kate called out. The woman did a lot of sewing for her grandchildren and was a good customer.

"Hello, Kate. I just stopped by to pick up some thread. I'm making pajamas for my grandsons for Christmas."

"I've got some great winter pajama fabric that just came in if you'd like to see it."

"Not today, I guess."

The woman went over to the thread and Kate saw

her slip a shopping bag out of her large carryall. She took out some fabric and began looking for thread to match. As the woman turned, Kate saw that the fabric bag said Fabulous Fabrics in bright red letters. The woman looked up and caught the expression on Kate's face.

"Fabulous Fabrics just opened today and they're having a half off sale that I just couldn't pass up," she explained apologetically.

Kate rang up the thread without speaking.

"You know when you get older you have to watch the pennies."

"I guess so," Kate said. She knew that Lucy often bragged about getting a new Cadillac every two years.

"I'm still going to buy some things here. You can't get personal attention in the big discount stores."

"That's true. And if you buy three dollars' worth of thread from me and twenty dollars' worth of fabric from them, eventually I'm going to go out of business," Kate said, handing the woman her bag.

The woman's mouth dropped open in surprise.

"I'm sorry," she said quickly, then she turned and practically ran out of the store.

Good going, Kate said to herself. *Embarrass your customers, that's a sure way to bring them rushing back. But what am I supposed to do? Some of them don't even realize the consequences of their behavior. All they want to do is save a nickel, even if it means that there'll be no one to give them advice when they need it.*

Kate grabbed the edge of the counter, feeling more desperate than she had since opening the store. What was she going to do? Fabulous Fabrics and handsome Roger were going to drive her out of business unless she could come up with some way of fighting back.

At seven o'clock the next morning Kate was out running. There had been no quilt classes the past night, so she'd eaten a good dinner and gone to bed early. The prospect of having Sandra to help out today had also given her a boost of energy.

How can a person not feel happy on a morning like this? Kate thought. It was early November. The mornings were crisp without being cold and the afternoons held enough warmth to make the prospect of winter still seem far away. Most of the leaves had fallen, but a few survivors clung stubbornly to the branches. *Hanging in there just like Golden Needles,* Kate defiantly told herself. Feeling a rush of confidence, she put on a burst of speed as she turned the corner from her street onto a more traveled road. It felt good to be moving her body, to be accomplishing something.

Kate never saw what happened: one minute she was charging happily through a pile of leaves in the gutter, the next minute she had slipped and fallen hard on her backside. As she went down she felt her left ankle twist to one side.

She sat there for a moment too stunned to move and feeling vaguely embarrassed at lying on her back by the side of the road. Finally, when she had found the courage to discover what still worked, she struggled to her feet. Gingerly she stepped on her left foot. A sharp surge of pain warned her that she wasn't going to be able to walk on it.

I guess I can hop home on my right foot, she thought, and began jumping on one foot in the direction of her apartment. But by the time she had hopped ten feet, her right leg had cramped up and she had to stop to rest. Now that the initial shock was wearing off, the pain in her injured ankle was starting to travel up her leg in waves. Kate sat down on the curb and leaned her head against a tree. *After a short rest, I'll try again,* she promised herself.

A green car pulled up to the curb just past her and the door opened. Out of the corner of her eye she saw a man get out. *Great,* Kate thought, *this is just what I need to be doing right now, fending off some strange guy who may or may not be a good Samaritan.*

"What's wrong?" Roger said, rushing to her side.

She tried to keep from shouting "hallelujah" at the sight of him. "I was running and twisted my ankle," Kate answered.

Roger gently lifted her leg.

"Can you move your foot?" he asked.

Kate slowly rotated her foot from side-to-side.

"Good. Probably it's not broken, but we should get it x-rayed just in case." He looked over at the pile of leaves. "Did you run through that?"

Kate nodded.

He shook his head as if she were crazy. "Wet leaves can be very slippery."

A wave of nausea came over Kate. "Can we save the object lesson until after I get some treatment?"

Roger grinned and nodded. "Stand up and lean on me. We'll go to the hospital emergency room."

Kate put her left arm over Roger's shoulder, thinking he was going to help her hobble along. With one quick movement he swept her up into his arms. Kate relaxed, letting her weight shift toward his chest. As he slowly carried her to the passanger side of the car, she felt safe and secure in a way she hadn't known for years. *Don't be silly, Kate,* she warned herself. *You can't depend on anybody but yourself. And you certainly can't depend on the manager of Fabulous Fabrics.* He placed her down briefly on her good foot, keeping his arm around her, then opened the door and carefully lifted her onto the seat.

"How did you happen to be passing by?" Kate asked faintly as another wave of pain washed over her.

"I was on my way to work early today and decided to take the scenic route. Guess it was your lucky day," he said, smiling.

Kate tried to smile back.

The emergency room was virtually empty when they arrived, November mornings apparently not being a prime time for crimes or accidents. Before Kate could object, the nurse who showed her into the treatment room encouraged Roger to come along. After a surprisingly uncomplicated trip to the x-ray room, she was whisked back to the treatment room where a young doctor examined the ankle.

"It isn't broken, but you've definitely strained the ligaments." The doctor looked over at Roger. "You should see that the ankle gets soaked in very cold water for at least twenty minutes. Then wrap it in an elastic bandage. Don't let her put any weight on the foot for a day or two. She can take some over-the-counter pain killers when she needs to."

"Hello," Kate was about to say. "I'm right here."

"Don't worry, doctor, I'll take care of it," Roger intoned solemnly before she could speak.

Kate wanted to object by telling the doctor that she was perfectly capable of taking care of herself, but a nurse immediately shoved a couple of tablets and a glass of water into her hand and ordered her to take them. Then the nurse reappeared with a wheelchair, and Kate was rolled out the door to Roger's car.

Kate gave Roger directions to her house, then leaned her head back against the headrest.

"I don't like it when people talk as if I'm not there or as if I'm too stupid to understand what they're saying."

"You mean the doctor."

"And you. It was like listening to the two big mature men decide how to put this stupid little girl back together."

"I think the doctor just assumed that I was your boyfriend or something. I didn't think it was the right time to tell him that I'm your fiercest competitor and would probably take this opportunity to push you down the stairs."

Kate laughed briefly. "Okay, you're doing me a big favor, so I shouldn't be irritable. But you can just leave me off at home, I'll take care of it from here. I have an elastic bandage from the last time Rhonda sprained her wrist lifting her sewing machine."

By the time they pulled up in front of her house, the worst of the pain had subsided. But now the ankle felt stiff like it wasn't even a part of her.

"Do you live on the first or second floor?" Roger asked.

"Second," Kate said. She visualized climbing the long, steep stairway which suddenly seemed about as doable to her as reaching the summit of Everest.

Roger glanced over at her. "How about we make a deal? I'll carry you up the stairs and chill down your ankle before it swells. In exchange, the next time I ask you to dinner you'll say 'yes'."

"That's blackmail," Kate said.

"Actually, it's extortion," Roger said with a grin. "But is it a deal?"

"A real gentleman wouldn't take advantage of a lady in distress," Kate said only half-seriously, knowing she sounded like every southern belle who'd ever lost her plantation.

"But I'm not a gentleman, am I? I'm your worst enemy. You've said as much yourself. So why shouldn't I try to take advantage of you?"

She looked into his blue eyes that were dancing with amusement and something more.

"Okay," she said. "You've got a deal."

Once again Roger lifted her into his arms as if she were weightless and carried her up on the porch. She fished the key out of the pocket of her running jacket, and he opened the door. He paused for a moment and stared up the long steep flight of stairs to the second floor.

"What's the matter? Don't you think you can make it?" Kate teased.

"If I lose my balance, I may have to drop you to save myself," he replied with a smile.

"Remember, as my number-one competitor, the police will come looking for you first if anything happens to me."

Roger grunted and started up the stairs. Kate pressed her ear against his chest to listen to his heart. The beat was deep and strong, only getting slightly more rapid as he reached the top. He managed to open the upstairs door with Kate in his arms, then he carried her inside and put her down on a straight chair in the living room. Like a bride being carried across the threshold, Kate thought, and shook her head to chase the idea away.

"You'd better get out of those," Roger said, gesturing toward her black Lycra running pants.

"Excuse me. You're only going to soak my foot and ankle. I can always pull up the leg of the pants." Kate reached down to demonstrate and immediately found that she couldn't get the elastic cuff above her rapidly swelling ankle.

"There's no time to waste," Roger said crisply. "Get into something else while I start putting ice in a bucket. You do have a bucket, don't you?"

"Under the sink," Kate directed. She leaned on the furniture for support and hopped toward her bedroom. "And there should be plenty of ice in the freezer."

Kate closed the door and listened to the sound of Roger making noises in the kitchen. There was something strangely satisfying about hearing him in the house. Something that made her feel less lonely.

Chapter Five

"Ohhh," Kate cried. She tried to lift her foot out of the bucket, but Roger gently pushed it back down again.

"You've got to keep the ankle submerged in order to do any good."

"Does it have to be so cold?"

"I'm only following the doctor's orders," he replied.

Kate stared down at the top of Roger's head as he bent over the bucket in which her foot was firmly placed. The fact that he was down on one knee made the scene seem positively medieval. The loyal knight paying homage to his lady. She had to admit that there was something rather romantic about having a man at her feet. Kate had always thought her girlfriends, who felt there was nothing greater than having a man down on bended knee proposing, were being rather silly, and

43

here she was getting a rush of pleasure at seeing a man in a somewhat similar position.

That'll teach me to get too uppity, Kate thought.

The water started to become a bit warmer as the ice melted. Kate closed her eyes and began to relax into the experience.

"Ohhh," she screamed again as Roger dumped more ice cubes into the water.

"Can't let it get warm," he said grinning up at her.

"I think you're enjoying this," she said.

"Well, it isn't often that a man gets to hold a woman's naked foot without having to buy her dinner first."

"Don't go getting any ideas," she warned. "The left knee is as far as I go on a first date." She was wearing a pair of loose-fitting jeans and had rolled the pants leg up to just above her shin.

"I didn't realize that I had permission to go that far," Roger said. He reached up to her calf and his strong fingers began to massage her tight calf muscle.

"Whoa!" Kate said, squirming for a moment. "That tickles."

Then suddenly it didn't tickle any more, and she closed her eyes as the tension began to drain out of her leg.

As his hands kneaded her leg, she felt a sense of warmth travel up her thigh. It was more than just strong hands relieving the stiffness in tight muscles; it was as if years of anxiety and stress were being loosened and released from her body. She let her head hang back against the upper rung of the high-backed kitchen chair. Just as his grip became painful he would pause, and the wave of release that swept over her as her muscles relaxed almost made her gasp.

She looked down at Roger and at the same time he looked up at her. His blue eyes were serious.

"That's enough for now," he said.

"Enough what?" Kate asked breathlessly.

"Enough cold water," he replied, lifting her foot out of the bucket. He wrapped the foot in a towel and began to carefully dry it. When he was done, Roger studied the ankle.

"What do you say, doc?" Kate asked.

"It's swollen, but still lovely," he said, giving her a mock lascivious grin. "We'll put an elastic bandage on it. Can you sit down at the store? You've got to stay off your feet, remember."

"I suppose . . . what time is it?" Kate asked, suddenly realizing that she'd lost all track of time this morning and the store had to open by ten.

"Nine-thirty."

Kate immediately tried to stand. "I've got to get dressed and get to the shop."

Roger motioned for her to sit down. "I can see you're going to be a problem patient. We have to wrap that foot first, then I'll take you to work."

Before Kate could object, Roger seized her foot and began wrapping the elastic bandage around it in a neat figure eight pattern.

"You've done this before," Kate said.

"College wrestling. All sorts of body parts get twisted and pulled. You spend half your time getting wrapped or helping to wrap someone else."

"What did you study in college?" Kate asked.

"I majored in studio art," Roger said, putting a clip on the elastic bandage to hold it in place. "I thought I was going to be a painter. The next Picasso, maybe."

"What happened?" Kate smiled to herself at the thought that she had started out as the hardheaded business major, and Roger had begun as the artist. Talk about positions being reversed.

"I needed to earn money. The idea of becoming a starving artist is romantic until you think seriously about the 'starving' part. But I was able to use my art background to get a job in textile design."

"Then why," Kate began slowly, not anxious to spoil the friendly mood of the moment, "did you ever go to work as a manager for Fabulous Fabrics?"

Roger laughed shortly. "I needed to earn a better salary. My father died a year after I finished college. My mom needed help to send my brother to college, and I've got two sisters who will be going in the next two years. My folks had paid my way, so I figured the least I could do was to help out. Fabric design was a lot of fun, but working for Fabulous Fabrics pays more."

"It's too bad you have to do something you don't enjoy."

"I do enjoy the business, but I also miss the chance to use my artistic side. Now let's get you to work."

Kate found that the bandage helped relieve the pain in her ankle as long as she limited the pressure on it. Putting most of her weight on her right foot, she carefully hopped into the bedroom. Not bothering to change her jeans, she slipped into a loose-fitting sweater. She found a pair of low-cut canvas shoes that didn't reach her ankle. Lacing one on her right foot, she kept the shoe on her left foot loose so her bandaged foot would fit inside.

"I peeked in your living room and saw that quilt on the sofa. Did you make that?" Roger asked as she came out of the bedroom.

Kate nodded. "I'm almost done hand quilting it. I plan to enter it in the Christmas Eve Quilt show."

"Where did you get fabrics with such wonderful colors?"

"I painted them myself. I took several classes on it from experts, and I thought I'd give it a try."

Roger stood for a moment, thinking.

"Is that something that could be done commercially? I mean, could you paint yards of fabric and sell it as a speciality item?"

"Oh, sure. A couple of people already do it by mail order and sell at quilt shows. There's a big demand for hand-painted fabrics."

"Maybe you should consider doing it yourself. You have a talent for it."

"I've never thought about it," Kate said, feeling as though a door had been opened.

"Might be worth considering. Well, are you ready for the trip down?" Roger asked, putting his arm around her. It felt surprisingly natural to Kate.

"I can probably walk now with my foot bandaged."

"Nonsense. You paid for a round trip, and I always make good on my deals."

He lifted her easily into his arms and looked down into her eyes.

"Ready?" he asked with a smile.

Kate arched her neck up and kissed him softly on the cheek. She let her lips linger a bit too long.

"You picked a dangerous time to make my knees turn to water, lady," Roger said. "We could both end up hurt."

He's right, Kate thought, jolted back to reality by the word "hurt." *What am I doing? Just because he helped me out, I'm letting my feelings get in the way of my good sense. He's going to put me out of business whether he wants to or not. I'll end up losing the one thing I've worked hard for the last three years. There's no way any kind of relationship is going to survive that. Why begin something that's only going to end in tears and recriminations?*

"Let's get going," she said in an angry tone.

Giving her a perplexed look due to the sudden change in mood, Roger carried her down the stairs and seated her in the car.

"I can pick you up after work and do this all over again if you'd like," Roger said.

"No need," Kate replied shortly. "I can lean on the banister and make it up the stairs with my ankle bandaged."

"How will you get home without a car?"

"I have a new part-time employee showing up this afternoon. She can give me a ride."

They made the rest of the trip to the shop in silence. When they got to the store, he opened the passenger door but before he could lift her out Kate was on her feet leaning against the side of the car.

"I can make it," she said, gasping as she absentmindedly rested her injured foot on the ground.

"Are you sure?" Roger asked, his face showing his concern.

"Positive. And about that dinner invitation—" Kate began.

"I was only kidding. I wouldn't hold you to a promise made under duress," Roger said quickly.

"I keep my promises," Kate replied. "As soon as I can walk around better, I'll be in touch."

"Fine. Take care of that ankle, Kate," Roger said, still seeming a bit bewildered at her change of attitude.

She nodded briefly, then turned to open the door to her shop.

Chapter Six

Kate watched Sandra, or Sandy, as she'd happily insisted that she wanted to be called, cut three yards of fabric for a customer. She clearly had a great deal of experience and her cheerful attitude would fit in well. Kate knew that sometimes she was too serious with customers, while Rhonda was often too vague. A happy, efficient employee would certainly be an asset. Perhaps she could find some way to keep Sandy after Rhonda returned.

"I'm going in the back room to do some paperwork. If you have any questions, give me a shout," Kate said once she and Sandy were alone in the shop.

"Great!" Sandy replied, giving her a thumbs-up sign.

Smiling to herself at all that energy, Kate hobbled into the back room and sank down into her old leather desk chair. She turned over an empty waste basket and propped her left foot up on it.

"This ankle doesn't make me feel a day over ninety," she grumbled to herself.

She pulled the morning paper over to her and looked again at the Fabulous Fabrics ad. ALL FABRICS 50% OFF OUR ALREADY INCREDIBLY LOW PRICES. The words strutted across the top of the full-page advertisement that Kate knew must cost five hundred dollars for a week's run. That was her advertising budget for six months. How could she compete with a store that could undersell her forever and proudly let the public know about it every day of the week?

Kate picked up a pad, her hands shaking with anger as she began to compose her own ad. DON'T BE FOOLED BY CLAIMS OF GIANT RETAILERS: BUY QUALITY FABRICS AT GOLDEN NEEDLES. In smaller print she went on to suggest that oftentimes fabrics purchased at a lower price were inferior to the goods sold in smaller fabric shops.

When Kate was done, she looked over her work and smiled. A quarter-of-a-page advertisement running for three days, *that* she could afford. Maybe she would be driven out of business, but she wouldn't go without a fight. She put the ad copy in an envelope. *I'll get this over to the Hampden County Record by this afternoon. That way it would run over the weekend,* Kate thought.

Filled with determination, she got up from her desk and groaned out loud when her left foot hit the floor.

Still gasping, she limped out into the retail area just

in time to hear Sandy say to a customer, "We don't have it in blue. You might try up the road at Fabulous Fabrics."

The customer thanked Sandy and left the shop.

"Sandy," Kate could hear her voice snap like a whip. *Stay calm,* she warned herself, *the girl has just started.*

"Hi, Kate," Sandy said bouncing over to the counter.

"Sandy, I don't want to hear you ever again send a customer to Fabulous Fabrics."

Sandy's face fell. "She asked me if I knew where she could get that fabric in blue. We don't have it, so I figured—"

"I'll give you a list of other quilt stores in the area. You can send customers to any one of those, but not to Fabulous Fabrics. Okay?"

Sandy nodded.

Kate smiled and touched Sandy on the shoulder. "I know you don't realize it, but that store could easily put us out of business, so I can't afford to give them any free publicity."

Sandy's cheerful look returned. Kate handed her the envelope with the ad in it.

"Would you run this over to the Hampden County Record? They're about a mile up the road on the left-hand side. You can't miss them. Give it to the man at the advertising desk."

"Sure. I'm right on it." She grabbed her nylon wind-breaker from the clothes tree and rushed out the door.

Kate hopped over to the counter and collapsed on a stool. She rested her head in her hands. The ankle was starting to really throb now. She'd forgotten to bring any pain killers, and Kate knew there were none in the shop. Rhonda believed only in natural remedies.

Kate smiled to herself. If Rhonda were here now, she'd have her chewing some kind of root that would turn her tongue black without doing a thing for the pain in her leg. But at least if Rhonda were here there would be somebody to talk to, somebody who cared about the shop as much as she did. Keeping all her worries pent up inside was just making her irritable. She couldn't go on flying off the handle with the customers or Sandy. She was rapidly becoming the kind of person she didn't like.

The bell over the door rang. Kate looked up, hoping it was Roger but at the same time telling herself not to be silly. Jack Martinson, her landlord and the owner of the mall, walked into the shop. Kate immediately tried to look happy and prosperous. A thin, nervous, middle-aged man, Jack was constantly worried about business. He was particularly concerned over whether two young women could make a success of a shop and, most important to him, could continue to pay the rent on time.

"Hello, Kate," he said, glancing around the store and frowning when he didn't see any customers. "How are things going?"

"Great," Kate said, knowing she sounded as maniacally upbeat as Sandy. She hoped Jack didn't know Fabulous Fabrics had opened, otherwise he'd already be searching for a new tenant to replace her.

"I just wanted to let you know that Prehistoric Platters is going out of business at the end of the month, so their space will be vacant."

That was the shop next door. Its owner had been in business just six months and Kate had looked in the place only once, but she knew he had a huge inventory of vinyl from the fifties, sixties, and early seventies. He also carried those little 45s and a lot of early tapes. She thought it was a clever idea, but you'd have to sell a lot of merchandise to meet the rent. Even older people were into CDs today.

"I'm sorry to hear that."

"Yeah. Louie is pretty broken up about it."

Kate had usually seen Louie, a round man with a full beard, sitting by the front window of the shop with a headset on and a mellow smile on his face. It was hard to imagine him getting very distressed about anything.

"It's hard to take a hobby and turn it into a business," Martinson said, giving her a meaningful look.

"You certainly need to know what you're doing," she replied, refusing to take the bait.

"Well, anyway, since Louie is leaving, I wanted you to know that I'll let you rent his space as well for two hundred more a month. He's got sort of a small area. Nobody wants stores with that kind of floor space anymore. We'd put the two spaces together." He made a kind of crunching motion with his hands.

"You'd combine the shops?"

He walked over and stared at the wall that held her supply rack.

"Yeah. This isn't a bearing wall, so we could just

knock it out and have a larger space that would be easier to rent."

"I'm not sure I can afford an increase in rent right now," Kate said. Her heart was pounding; she wasn't even sure she could still afford the current rent.

Jack shrugged. "It's up to you. You have what, three more months on your lease? After that the two spaces get combined whether you're interested or not. If you can afford it, I'd be happy to rent to you. If you can't, I'll find somebody else who can. Nothing personal, you understand, it's just business. This mall costs me a fortune."

Although she guessed that Jack was making plenty on the rents, Kate stayed silent.

"Plus there are those skateboarders." Martinson shook his head in disgust.

A small group of skateboarders gathered after school and well into the evening every day in front of a pizzeria several doors down where they would practice boarding on the smooth cement walk. They usually didn't come down as far as Kate's because they liked to jump up on the wall of the decorative flower planter in front of Prehistoric Platters, and very few of them were able to make it along the top of the wall without falling. Still, the noise of their wheels and the ever-present possibility that they would crash into one of her older customers worried Kate a little, but she thought Jack exaggerated the situation.

"Yeah. There's always them," Kate said.

"And the police won't do anything about it," Jack added as he stuck an antacid into his mouth and gave the shop a critical once-over. "Give my offer some thought. You won't get a better location."

"I'll consider it," Kate said coolly. Jack was at his most annoying when he pretended to care about his tenants, for she knew he was concerned solely with getting the maximum rent.

The afternoon seemed endless. Sandy finally returned and apologized for being late. She'd missed the newspaper building twice and gotten lost. Kate told her to hold the fort and went in the back room. She pulled out the books for the last two years and tried to come up with a prediction about how business would be for the rest of the year.

If Fabulous Fabrics weren't part of the equation, they might have been able to rent the additional space based on the reasonable hope that business would coninue to improve as it had for the past twenty-four months. *But that blasted Fabulous Fabrics,* Kate thought to herself. There was no way she could safely assume that the future would be as rosy as the past. Roger's face came into her mind, and she was overwhelmed by two conflicting emotions. Could you love and hate a person at the same time? She was starting to think it was possible.

By quarter to five, Kate was ready to do what she almost never did: close early. Her ankle was throbbing and her head wasn't far behind. A light rain had started to fall and only a truly desperate or dedicated quilter would come out in the early darkness to buy fabric.

"Let's cut out early," Kate said to Sandy, whom she'd already asked for a ride home.

They locked the back door and turned out the lights. Kate went first out the front door. She took a few steps away from the door and turned as she fished the key out of her jacket pocket. All she heard was a shout and suddenly a body slammed hard into hers and she went crashing back onto the sidewalk with someone on top of her.

For the second time that day, Kate lay on her back mentally checking her body parts and waiting to gain her composure before attempting to stand.

"Are you all right, lady?" a worried voice asked.

Kate focused her vision on a skinny boy in a loose sweatshirt and baggy pants who was standing over her holding a skateboard in one hand.

"Let me help you," Sandy shouted, pushing the boy out of the way. She reached down and began pulling frantically on Kate's right arm.

"Thanks, Sandy, but let me do it myself," Kate said.

Slowly putting her right knee on the ground, Kate carefully stood, reaching her left arm out to Sandy for support so her bad foot wouldn't hit the ground. The boy's eyes widened in fright as he saw how hard it was for her to get to her feet. Kate smiled.

"You didn't do all this damage. I already had a sprained ankle."

"You could have been killed!" Sandy shouted. "We should call the police and get an ambulance. You might have broken bones that you don't even know about yet."

Kate leaned against a post and handed Sandy the key. "Would you lock the door for me? I only had the wind knocked out of me. Otherwise I'm okay."

"This is what happens when you guys skateboard where people are walking," Sandy scolded.

The boy looked contrite, but three others standing a few yards behind smirked.

"It was an accident. I never thought I'd get to the end of the wall," the boy said. "I never have before."

"Way to go, Tim," one of his friends called.

"None of them have either," Tim said with a glimmer of pride. "But I'm really sorry that I ran into you."

"No problem," Kate said, grinning. "And congratulations. I'm glad that I could make your landing a little softer."

The boy flashed a dazzling smile. He gave her a small wave and turned to go back to his friends.

Holding on to Sandy, Kate made her way to the car.

"I still think you should have called the police. You could have been badly injured," said Sandy, glaring at the boys as she drove out of the parking lot.

Kate began to shake her head, then changed her mind. Every part of her body hurt right now, including her neck.

"All my landlord needs is to have me calling the police to his precious mall. He'd probably find some way to break my lease and throw me out so he could get more rent."

"That's terrible," Sandy said.

Kate stared out the window and watched the raindrops travel down the glass. She couldn't disagree.

After a supper of tomato soup and a toasted American cheese sandwich, comfort food from her childhood, Kate took a couple of aspirin and a long, hot relaxing bath. Afterwards most of her muscles stopped hurting, at least momentarily. Wrapped in a quilt her mother had made, she lay on the sofa. What was she going to do about the shop? She tried to think about it calmly.

David may have been lucky enough to beat Goliath by going head-to-head against him but that isn't going to work for me, Kate thought. *I've got to find an angle, something that I can offer customers that Fabulous Fabrics can't or won't.*

Her eyes drifted to the foot of the sofa where the quilt she was working on was neatly folded. Would fabric painting really be something she could do commercially as Roger had suggested? She had enjoyed what she had done so far, mixing the colors and watching them form intricate patterns on the plain cotton or silk, putting objects on top of the painted material so the sun would form varying images of light and dark.

She had enjoyed it so much that she hardly thought of it as work. Work was running the shop, managing the inventory, paying the bills, calculating the taxes, keeping Rhonda on target, and dealing with the day-to-day needs of her customers. Art wasn't work, it was play.

She shook her head. Except for someone like Rhonda, who only occasionally knew which way was up, you couldn't go through life doing something that you actually enjoyed. Play was play and work was work.

The phone rang. Kate picked it up, hoping the call had nothing to do with the shop. Quilters sometimes

called her and Rhonda at home if they got into trouble
with a project and needed advice.

"Hello, Katie. Just thought I'd check and see how
life is treating you."

Although Kate would never have called her mother
to complain about a difficult day, the temptation from
hearing her voice on the phone was overwhelming.
While not mentioning the seriousness of her financial
situation, Kate told her mother about the opening of
Fabulous Fabrics, her various meetings with Roger
and Melissa, her sprained ankle, and Rhonda's visit to
California.

"Sounds like that young man did just fine with that
drunk."

"He did just fine with my ankle too," Kate said,
smiling contentedly to herself. She had left out the part
about the calf massage. Some things her mother didn't
have to know.

"You've got to be careful with a sprain like that. It
was nice of him to take the time to help you. You say
that he keeps asking you out."

"Yeah, but he's the competition. You know what
they say about keeping business and pleasure separate."

Her mother chuckled. "Katie, sometimes I think
you're the mother and I'm the child. You sound older
than I do."

"What do you mean?"

"Circumstances change, character doesn't. It's only
by circumstance that he's your competitor, that may
not last forever. If he's a good man, you should give

him a chance. Anyway, you promised that you'd go out to dinner with him."

"But he let me take back my promise," Kate pointed out.

Kate could envision her mother shaking her head on the other end of the line.

"You gave your promise. Now if you don't want to go out to dinner with him alone, you know there is an occasion coming up at the end of the month."

"Thanksgiving?"

"Why don't you invite him to come up here with you?"

"I don't think so," Kate said without thinking. You just don't bring a man home to meet Mom the first time you go out with him. Either you'll scare him away or you'll never get rid of him. "Anyway, I usually stay over for a couple of days."

"Well, you think about it, Katie. You could always go back the same day if that's the problem. After all, you'll be up to stay over for Christmas a few weeks later. There will be plenty of food, and it might be kind of nice to have someone here besides just the two of us."

"Okay, I'll think about it." *But I'm not about to do it,* she thought to herself.

Chapter Seven

The paper boy came into Golden Needles and put Kate's Friday paper on the counter. She'd been waiting four days for this: the chance to see her advertisement in print. She tore through the paper searching, until she spotted the quarter-page ad on the bottom of page twelve. As she read through the text of the advertisement, Kate could feel herself begin to blush.

She thought she had pointed out that small quilt stores provided consistently high quality materials for a fair price, while discount stores often carried goods of lower quality for bargain prices. She had warned that many less expensive fabrics did not always materialize into the kind of finished items that a real craftsperson would be proud of showing. She had also emphasized that the knowledgeable sales people at most quilt stores could provide expert help in making selections, whereas many discount stores had inexperienced employees who were often too busy to be of help.

But the advertisement was almost an accusation that discount stores lied about the quality of the goods they sold—that they mislabeled products in order to intentionally deceive customers, and that they hired employees who made no effort at customer service. Had she actually said all those things? She knew that she'd been angry when she composed the ad, but it had seemed much more moderate at the time.

The bell over the door rang, and Kate automatically looked up hoping that it would be Roger. It was. Her heart leaped until she saw the grim expression on his face. Before the door could close Melissa came tearing in behind him. She walked up to the counter and slapped a copy of the newspaper down on the counter in front of Kate.

"Did you write this?" Melissa demanded.

"Yes, I guess I did." Kate knew that sounded weak, but somehow the words of the ad seemed strange to her. Like somehow the bad Kate had taken over her body and written it in a fit of nastiness.

Melissa leaned over the counter toward her until Kate could smell her expensive scent.

"We're going to sue. You can bet on it. And when we're done not only will this shop be closed, but you are personally going to owe us millions in damages."

Kate pressed her lips together so they wouldn't tremble. It was one thing to be in trouble because of circumstances; it was another to make a mistake this serious. She looked at Roger.

"Okay, Melissa, you've made your point," he said

calmly. "Now why don't you wait in the car for a few minutes while I talk to Kate."

"Don't back down on this, Roger. My—"

"Wait in the car, Melissa. I'll be right out," Roger said, cutting her off.

With a toss of her hair, Melissa turned and marched out of the shop.

Roger sighed. "Why did you do this, Kate?"

Kate would have felt better if he had sounded angry or bitter. The disappointment in his voice really hurt.

She shook her head. "I saw your ad in the paper and I wanted to respond. I guess I got carried away and said more than I should have. I'm sorry."

Roger stared off across the shop.

"You know, Melissa is right. This does come very close to being libelous. You virtually accuse us of consumer fraud."

"I didn't mean to," Kate blurted out.

Roger smiled slightly. "I believe you, and I can understand that our coming into town had gotten you very upset. So upset that you might have written something that you otherwise wouldn't have."

"I could print a retraction in the paper. I could admit that I exaggerated."

"No. That would just draw more attention to the whole thing. I think it would be best if we just let the matter slide. We'll forget that it ever happened. Probably most people didn't bother to read the small print in your ad anyway, so it won't hurt our business."

"You won't sue me?" Kate asked.

Roger shook his head, then he grinned. "Not this time, anyway. But if you do it again . . ."

Kate took a deep breath and crossed her heart. "I promise I won't."

"Okay, then."

"But what about Melissa? She seems pretty intent on taking me to court."

"I run the store," Roger said, almost too firmly. He paused and went on more gently. "Melissa might like to sue, but I can make her see that having Fabulous Fabrics haul a small shop owner into court is hardly going to get us good publicity or endear us to the quilting community."

Maybe not, Kate thought, *but getting rid of me would certainly bring joy to her heart.*

"How's the ankle?" Roger asked.

"It feels a little better every day."

"Keep taking care of it," he said softly.

Kate stared into his blue eyes and remembered how upset she had felt a few moments ago when he'd come into the store and been so clearly disappointed in her. It wasn't just the loss of the store that had worried her, she realized, but the loss of Roger's good opinion of her. She really cared what he thought of her.

"I guess I still owe you a dinner," Kate said.

Roger waved his hand. "I've already let you off the hook on that one."

"You've already helped me three times: with the drunk, with my ankle, and now with this. It's the least I can do."

"I don't want you to go out with me out of some sense of obligation," Roger said. "I'd like you to go out with me because you think you'd enjoy it."

The sadness and longing suddenly revealed in his expression made Kate catch her breath.

"I'm not reluctant because I think I wouldn't enjoy dinner with you."

"I know. It's because I'm the enemy," he said wearily.

Kate frowned. Perhaps all this talk of being enemies was as silly as her mother had suggested. Roger had proven himself to be a nice guy who cared about her. Why let circumstances dictate whether they became friends?

"But let's see," Kate said, "Thanksgiving is a week away. Now if the pilgrims and the Indians could get together for Thanksgiving and have a good time, I think friendly enemies like us should be able to as well. If you're free, that is."

A smile lit up Roger's face. "My family lives out near Chicago, so I wasn't planning to go home this year. That would be great. So I'll get to meet your family?"

"My Mom. That's all there is. She lives in southern Vermont, right across the state line. We'll go up and come back the same day."

"Fine. I'll call you next week and we can work out the details."

He reached across the counter and gently brushed the back of his fingers along Kate's cheek. Her vision blurred. She wanted to grab his hand and cover it with kisses.

"Thanks, Kate," he said. "Thanks for giving us a chance."

Before she realized it he had left the store.

Kate put her elbows on the counter and rested her head in her hands. *Am I losing it?* she wondered. *First, I write that crazy ad, then I actually do what my mother wants and invite the competition home for dinner. What next? Maybe Melissa and I will get together and take in a movie like best girlfriends. Nah,* Kate decided, *that would be too weird.*

The phone rang.

"Hi. It's me," a familiar voice said when Kate answered.

"Rhonda! How are you? How's your mother?"

"She's doing fine."

"Are you making meals for her and driving her places?" Kate asked.

There was a long pause. "Well, actually, I'm not staying with her right now. I was there for the first few days, but then Mom got me a job house sitting for some people she knows a few blocks away."

Kate smiled to herself. So even Rhonda's mother couldn't take her daughter's constant attention for very long.

"Are you coming back soon?" Kate asked. "I've got a lot to tell you about what's been happening here."

"Well, you see I've . . . I've met a guy."

"Good for you. Make sure you take a picture of him to bring back with you."

Rhonda was always meeting men and instantly falling in love. After one or two dates, something would happen and they would break up. Kate almost never got to meet any of them, so Rhonda's references to men in her past were hard to keep straight. Maybe a picture would help.

"Uh, that's the thing. I don't know exactly when I'll be coming back."

"I thought you said that your Mom was doing fine."

"Oh, she is, but you see, this guy, Travis, and I, well, we're talking about getting married."

"Talking about?" Kate asked. She wondered how people discussed something like that in the abstract. Of course, with Rhonda anything was possible.

"Yes. We're talking about getting married on February fourteenth. That's Valentine's Day, you know?"

"I know," Kate said dully.

"That was Travis's idea. He's so romantic. He even wants us to get married on the beach—using our own vows."

"I see."

"Kate?"

"Hmm?"

"Would you be my bridesmaid?"

"I guess . . . of course I will," Kate replied. Rhonda sounded so vulnerable and afraid that Kate decided she'd find the money for the trip somewhere.

"One other thing, Kate. Travis makes surfboards and he doesn't have a lot of money just yet. So we are going to need the money I've got invested in the shop to get started out here. Things are so expensive."

Kate sighed. "You know how the shop is doing, Rhonda. It's going to be real hard for me to come up with enough money to buy you out right now."

"Oh, I know, there's no rush. Maybe if you could have some of it by my wedding day. Travis would like us to go on a cruise for our honeymoon."

"I'll do what I can."

After several more minutes of talk about how wonderful Travis was with his bronzed body and blond hair, and how his surfboard business was sure to take off in the next year or two, Rhonda hung up.

How am I ever going to get the money to pay Rhonda for her share of the business? Kate thought. The way things were going there might not even be a Golden Needles by February. Another burden on her shoulders. Not only did she have to keep the shop going for herself, but she also had to keep it going so Rhonda could get married and settle down in California with beautiful golden Travis.

Of course, it was always possible that Travis would leave Rhonda and go wandering off in search of the perfect wave. *That would let me off the hook financially,* Kate thought, but she couldn't bring herself to wish that kind of disappointment on her friend.

The shop bell rang and Sandy came breezing through the door with a big smile.

"Hey, how's it going, Kate?"

Kate tried to give her an extra friendly smile. With Rhonda gone it looked like she and Sandy were going to have to get along for a long time.

Chapter Eight

*I*s *this trip to Vermont with Roger such a good idea?*
Kate asked herself as she thought about it more the
next day. Since they'd never had a conversation that
lasted for more than ten minutes, thanks largely to
Melissa, Kate wondered whether the hour-and-a-half
trip would be one long ordeal as they searched for
things to talk about. Or at least searched for things
that wouldn't bring to mind their unpleasantly com-
petitive situation.

We could just look at the view and not talk, Kate
thought, *but that would be pretty strange and uncomfortable. Maybe I should make up a list of possible
topics and memorize it before we go. That sounds like
something you'd do as a teenager going out on your
first date, yet in some ways I feel almost as nervous
as that. Why? Isn't Roger just another good-looking
guy? What makes him so special?*

She pulled into the parking lot in front of Golden Needles without having found an answer to that question. She got out of the car carrying a bag of equipment she'd need for the class she was teaching tonight. It was only when she stepped up on the sidewalk right in front of the door that she noticed. This couldn't be her shop. It didn't look the same. There was. . . .

SKATEBOARDERS RULE was written in red spray paint across the door. SKATEBOARDING ISN'T AGAINST THE LAW was sprayed across the window on the left. YOU LEAVE—NOT US it said across the right window.

It seemed as if, for one crazy moment, the store was moving toward her, attacking her. Kate stepped back, putting her weight on her left foot. Pain traveled up her leg and she leaned against the pillar supporting the overhang. Who had done this? And why? Was it because of the incident the other day with the skateboarder? It was true that Sandy had wanted to call the police, but Kate had vetoed the idea. Had those boys really been so outraged by a minor scolding that they would do this? Kate pictured the smiling boy who had crashed into her. He hadn't seemed nasty or vindictive, but then who could really understand a boy's mind?

With a deep sigh, Kate opened the door and went into the shop. At least none of the windows had been broken. She called Jack Martinson's number. He answered on the first ring. When she explained what had happened, he sputtered on about the evils of teenage boys in general and skateboarders in particular. Then, suddenly suspicious, he'd asked whether Kate had any problems with the boys lately. After Kate explained the incident of several days ago, Jack had the nerve to mumble something about women overreacting to boyish pranks. Then he said that he'd call the police and come over himself in a little while.

Just what I need, Kate thought to herself. *Now I've become the target of vandals. Knowing how protective and worried Jack is about his precious mall, he'll probably blame me, the victim, and be sure to want me out of here once my lease is up. One thing after another.* She felt like crying out of anger and frustration.

"A good cry every once in a while is okay. It lets out lots of bad feelings," her mother often said. "But do it on your own time, not when there's work to be done."

Kate went into the bathroom and washed her eyes with cold water. She combed her hair and decided that she looked weary but in charge, not bad for someone who'd just had her shop vandalized.

She was returning to the counter as a police cruiser pulled up in front; right behind was Martinson. The two men stood outside and studied the graffiti for a while as if it would somehow provide a clue to the perpetrator. Jack was gesturing the whole time while the police officer nodded and looked bored. Then they came into the shop. Kate repeated what she had told her landlord about the incident with the skateboarders. She tried not to express any opinion one way or the other about their possible guilt.

"It's got to be those kids," Jack said. "But they've been hanging around here for months. Why would they start doing something like this now?"

Kate shrugged.

"It must be that you or your helper said just the thing that set them off," he said, answering his own question. "Who knows where it will stop now? They could take it into their heads to spray paint all the shops, one window at a time. The place will look like a slum."

He popped an antacid tablet in his mouth and began crunching loudly. All the while he glared at Kate accusingly.

"You said that these kids usually come around at three o'clock?" asked the police officer.

Kate nodded. "Right after school, I guess. They stay until it gets dark."

The officer jotted something in a small spiral notebook. "Okay. I'll be back at four and talk with them. We can't prove that they did it, but if it was them, a good stern warning might put enough fear into them so that they won't try anything else. I'll also have a patrol car pull into the parking lot for the next few nights just to check on things."

As the policeman was leaving the shop, Roger rushed in.

"Are you all right, Kate?" he asked.

"Fine."

"I saw the police car outside, and I . . ."

Roger saw Jack and stopped.

"I know you," Martinson said. "It was at the last Chamber of Commerce meeting where they introduced new members. You're the guy who runs some new store."

"Roger Garrison. He's the manager of Fabulous

Fabrics." Kate said. "This is Jack Martinson, my land-lord."

Martinson shook hands with Roger and winked in Kate's direction.

"Pretty smart, young lady," he said. "It never hurts to stay in good with the competition just in case you need to get a new job."

Kate glared at the man, but he didn't seem to notice.

"Did you see what those kids did out there?" Jack said to Roger. Jack shook his head as if he didn't know what the world was coming to. "No upbringing, that's the problem. These kids have got no upbringing."

"Yeah, it's a shame," Roger said half-heartedly, risking a quick smile at Kate.

"Have you given any more thought to what I proposed about combining the shops?" Jack suddenly asked her out of the blue.

"I'll let you know closer to the end of my lease," Kate said shortly.

"Well, be thinking about it," he said in a tone full of warning. "I'll have my maintenance guys clean up the graffiti, but it might take until tomorrow." He gave Roger a wave and left the shop.

"Sorry I barged in like that, but when I saw the police car I was concerned that something really bad had happened."

"You don't think having your shop covered with spray paint is bad enough?" Kate snapped. Then she waved her hand. "Sorry, I know what you mean. You were afraid something had happened to me."

Roger smiled. "But I can see that I needn't have worried. You've got it all under control."

Kate nodded, wishing that it were true.

"I really am sorry that you have to put up with this kind of thing. Anybody in retail is at the mercy of every deadbeat who happens to walk by with a bad attitude," Roger said. "And when you have kids hanging around, then you only increase your likelihood for trouble."

They seemed like nice enough boys," Kate said.

"You can never tell."

"I guess so."

"By the way, I'm really looking forward to our Thanksgiving trip and dinner. I was wondering if there was anything you wanted me to bring."

"I guess not. I generally make a couple of pies, usually a pumpkin and a mince."

"And how are you going to do that what with working most nights and almost all day? Plus I'll bet that ankle still bothers you when you have to stand for a long time. Why don't you let me supply the pies?"

Kate looked doubtful.

"What's the matter? Don't you think I can tell the difference between pumpkin and lemon meringue?"

"It's not that. I'm sure you'd buy very good ones from the bakery, but it wouldn't be the same as homemade."

Roger reached across the counter and covered her hand. His blue eyes gazed into hers with mock anger.

"C'mon, Kate, do I look like the kind of guy who would try to foist off a bought pie on you and your mother? Will you trust me at least that much?"

Kate grinned. "Okay, but if you think I'm fussy

about pies, you should meet my mother. You're putting yourself into a dangerous situation."

Roger gave her a mysterious wink. "Don't worry, sweetheart. Danger is my business."

It was just after six and Kate was in the back room preparing for the evening's class when she heard the bell over the door. Sandy had left at five. Kate usually closed at six and reopened at seven when class began, but she'd been so busy preparing that she'd forgotten to lock the door.

"Sorry, we're not . . ." She stopped.

The boy from the other night stood in the middle of the shop holding his skateboard. He was shifting nervously from foot to foot.

"What can I do for you?" Kate asked, trying to sound friendly but formal. He didn't look dangerous, but you could never tell.

"We didn't do it, lady. We're not the ones who sprayed your shop."

"I didn't say you were," Kate replied.

"Yeah, well the cops think so. They just about accused us of doing it."

"That's because of what was written about skateboarding."

"Yeah, well anybody who knows we hang out here could have written that. It wasn't us."

"Okay. You've got a point. I don't know who did it. I'm not blaming you or your friends."

The boy nodded as if that seemed fair. "I'm Tim," he announced.

"I'm Kate."

"You know, I live right across the street," he said, pointing to a two-story house on the other side of the road. "I saw something last night."

"What?" Kate asked.

"I didn't pay much attention when it happened. But my bedroom is in the front of the house and at about eleven I looked out the window. I saw a red sports car parked right here in front of your shop. I only remembered because the car looked pretty neat."

"Could you see who was driving it?" Kate asked.

He shook his head. "I didn't really look. I just sort of wondered why it was there, that's all."

A red sports car, Kate thought. Now who did she know who owned one of those? But would Melissa really go as far as criminal mischief to destroy Golden Needles? Maybe not, but she might go that far to keep her away from Roger. And in Melissa's twisted mind anything that hurt Kate's business would keep her from getting involved with Roger.

"Thank you, Tim," Kate said. "You know, I definitely believe you now. I don't think you or your friends had anything to do with what happened."

The boy's smile lit up his face. "And don't worry, I'll keep an eye on the place for you, Kate. If I see anything strange happening I'll check it out."

"If you see anything, have your parents call the police," Kate said carefully.

"Sure thing," Tim said, and he gave her a wink of complicity.

What is it with men and winks? Kate wondered.

Chapter Nine

Kate was lost in thought the next morning as she drove to work. Would Melissa really do something so despicable, criminal actually, as vandalizing her shop? A person who would do that . . . Kate shivered . . . would do almost anything to get her way. She could talk to Roger about it, but all she had was the evidence of a boy who saw a red sports car in front of her shop. Would Roger be willing to confront Melissa on evidence as slim as that? For some reason he kept her as his assistant, even though she was obviously very emotional, so there must be some personal reason why he didn't fire her. That brought Kate back to the question of exactly what kind of relationship Roger and Melissa had, not a subject she cared to think about.

Trying to clear her mind of the whole thing, Kate began paying close attention to the road just in time to notice that the large gray corner house she went by every day had a FOR SALE sign in front of it. Kate knew that it was the former home of Dagmar's Dolls. She'd met Dagmar, a woman well into her sixties, a couple of years ago. When Golden Needles first opened Kate had made a point of going around and introducing herself to the owners of the various craft stores in the area.

Kate remembered that the house had an attractive retail space at the front of the first floor. In the back had been a large work area where Dagmar kept her kiln for firing porcelain dolls and a work area for students taking classes.

Because Kate expressed an interest in the house, which dated back to the late nineteenth century, Dagmar also had shown her the second and third floors which she used as a living area for herself and her husband. The house was huge with a living room, formal dining room, country kitchen, bathroom, and bedroom on the second floor and a rental apartment on the third. It was a wonderful house, and Kate had fallen in love with it immediately. The beautiful flat lawn and the large stately trees in the front of the property made it even more enticing.

When she'd heard that Dagmar and her husband were giving up the business and retiring to Florida, Kate had promised herself that she'd keep an eye on the property in case it went on the market. *Not that there's any way that I realistically can afford to buy a house,* Kate thought to herself. *But everyone is entitled to dream. Now it's finally on the market and will probably be snatched up by someone who will live there for the next twenty years.*

She sighed. *Well, there's no use worrying about things that are impossible to have. I've got enough problems hanging on to what I do have.* Even as she was telling herself this, Kate was memorizing the agency and the name of the realtor handling the house.

Kate spent the entire morning dreaming about the house between customers. The downstairs would be perfect for a sales space, and if she did go into fabric painting in a big way, the back room would be a wonderful work space. She could dry the fabric outside in the nice weather on tables set up on the lawn. She could live comfortably on the second floor and even rent out the third floor to pay the mortgage.

Just when she'd convince herself to pick up the phone and call the realtor, her sensible side would say that there was no way that she could afford it. Her business was on the brink of going bankrupt as it was, and this house, even if she could by any remote chance get a mortgage, would only pull her down faster. The struggle went back and forth for most of the morning.

Finally Kate remembered that her mother once said, "Your father and I would never have gotten this farm if we'd waited until we could really afford it. There always would have been something that made it risky. Finally we just had to take a chance and do it. I've never regretted that decision."

Kate made the call.

By the time Sandy came in at noon, Kate was pacing around the shop despite the occasional pain she still had in her left ankle. Her appointment wasn't until two, but now that she had made a decision Kate could hardly sit still.

Right behind Sandy came the delivery man with next month's fabric order from one of their major suppliers. Trying to keep her mind on business, Kate got her inventory sheet and quickly checked each item as it was carried into the store.

"There seems to be one bolt missing," Kate said when the man handed her the manifest to sign. "I ordered the Chinese Garden fabric."

The man looked down at his form and nodded. "Yep. Says here you ordered it a month ago, but it shows that you canceled the order two weeks ago."

"I did not cancel the order," Kate said firmly.

The man shrugged. "You'll have to call the office and work it out. I just deliver what they put on the truck."

Kate turned to Sandy as the man left.

"We have to have that fabric for the class I'm teaching on the Friday right after Thanksgiving. I'll have to get it somewhere."

"Fabulous Fabrics might have it," Sandy said brightly.

Kate gave her a stern look. "There are other places to try. But first I'm going to find out what happened with my order."

A call to Sam, her supplier, revealed that indeed someone had canceled the order by phone.

"Yeah, you called me," Sam said. "You told me that you wanted to cancel your order on the Chinese Garden fabric."

"Did I give you the invoice number?" Kate asked.

"C'mon, Kate," Sam said with a laugh. "I knew it

was you. Why would I go to the trouble of checking the invoice number?"

"Because it wasn't me, Sam."

There was a long pause. "You mean someone was sabotaging your order?"

"That's right. Did the woman sound like me?"

"I don't know. Maybe not. But there's a lot of noise around here, and I never would have expected anyone to pretend to be you. I mean . . ."

"Okay, okay. How soon can you get me the fabric?"

"We can rush order it and I can have it to you by Monday."

Kate sighed. "Don't bother, Sam. I'll try to buy some around here in time for my class on Friday."

"I'm really sorry about this, Kate. Do you have any idea who'd do something like this to you?"

"I'm not certain, but I have my suspicions."

"Well, the next time someone calls and tries to change your order, I'll be sure to check the invoice number."

"Thanks, Sam, I'd appreciate it."

Kate put down the phone and stared at her desk top. Melissa might have guessed that Kate would have an order in to one of the major suppliers. Heck, she could have called every major supplier until she found one who had an order from Golden Needles. But how would she know exactly which item to cancel in order to create the most havoc?

Kate reached across her desk and picked up the last schedule of classes that she'd sent out in September. There it was, right on the supply list for the Friday after Thanksgiving class: students are required to purchase two yards of Chinese Garden fabric on the day of the class. Melissa would also be able to easily discover who manufactured the fabric and when the deliveries would be arriving in this area. She'd know that if she canceled the order, it would be impossible for Kate to reorder the fabric in time.

I'm not going to let that drama queen get the better of me, Kate thought to herself. She picked up the phone and punched in the number for Quilter's Paradise, a store much like her own about ten miles away.

"Hi, Jen, this is Kate Manning. How's it going?"

"Okay."

She'd known Jen for several years and never heard her sound so restrained before. Maybe business was tough all over with Fabulous Fabrics in the area.

"Jen, I'm having a problem with an order for Chinese Garden fabric that I need for a class right after Thanksgiving. Do you have some?"

"Let me check."

Kate heard raised voices in the background but couldn't make out what they were saying. Finally, Sarah, Jen's partner, came on the line.

"Hi, Kate. How much do you need?"

"Ten or twelve yards."

"Sure, we've got it."

"Great, I'll be right over to pick it up."

"I'll be waiting for you," Sarah replied.

Kate grabbed her bag and went out into the shop. If she hurried, she could make it to Quilter's Paradise and still get to her realtor's appointment on time. Sandy was behind the counter and there were no customers in the shop.

"Hold the fort, Sandy. I'll be back by around three."

Sandy gave her a smile and a wave.

Quilter's Paradise was a small storefront in a row of shops in the downtown area of Northhampton. Not much to look at from the outside, it boasted over two thousand bolts of fabric which were stacked from floor to ceiling around the walls of the shop. The old wooden floors creaked as Kate walked up to the counter. Sarah, as good as her word, was behind the counter and had pulled out the bolt of Chinese Garden.

"Hi, Sarah," Kate said. "It's certainly a relief to see that you've got that fabric. You guys are a lifesaver."

Sarah didn't smile. "You said ten or twelve yards." She walked over to the cutting table.

"Twelve if you have it. Better to be on the safe side."

Sarah began to unwind the bolt of fabric.

"So how have things been?" Kate asked.

"Okay," Sarah said, concentrating on cutting the fabric as if she'd never done it before.

Since Sarah and Jen were usually full of cheerful conversation, Kate couldn't understand why Sarah was so subdued. Must be some personal problem, Kate concluded.

"Is Jen around?" Kate asked.

Sarah's head ducked slightly as if she were avoiding something unpleasant.

"She had to go out."

"How's business been?"

Sarah put down her scissors and stared at Kate, her lips formed a tight hard line.

"You have a lot of nerve asking me that."

"What do you mean?" Kate asked. She smiled, thinking that Sarah was joking, but the woman's expression didn't soften.

"You come in here all the time acting like our friend, and then you tell people to go to Fabulous Fabrics if they can't find what they want in your shop."

"What are you talking about?"

"Don't pretend that you don't know." Sarah stared at her, furious.

"Well, I don't," Kate said, realizing that she was getting angry herself.

Sarah's gaze faltered.

"Look, a woman was in the shop last week. She said that you told her that if Golden Needles didn't have what she was looking for, then she should go to Fabulous Fabrics. You told her that the manager there was a friend of yours, so you were passing on the business to them."

Kate was too stunned to speak.

"I thought all of us who owned small shops were going to stick together." Sarah's eyes filled with tears. "Business is tough enough without traitors."

"Who was this woman who told you that?" Kate asked.

"I'd never seen her before."

"Was she tall and thin, and did she look like a fashion model?" She'd kill Melissa yet.

Sarah shook her head. "No, she was short and not particularly thin."

Who could that be? Kate wondered. Was Melissa hiring people to spread false rumors about her?

Kate told Sarah about all the things that had been

happening recently. She explained her theory that Melissa was behind this campaign of sabotage. She told Sarah everything except her suspicion that at least part of Melissa's motive was jealousy over Roger. That was getting a little too personal, and Kate was not about to have people thinking of her as one side of an ugly love triangle.

When Kate was done, Sarah's eyes widened. "Do you really think she'd go that far just to put you out of business?"

"You haven't met her. She's very determined and more than a little unstable. But don't tell anyone but Jen what I've said. If the story gets around, Melissa will be threatening to sue me again, this time for slander."

"Okay. But maybe you should tell her boss. This guy may not know what she's doing. Maybe he could stop her."

"Good idea," Kate said.

But would Roger believe her? She could imagine him giving her an analytical look and wanting to see some hard evidence. Aside from a red sports car spotted by a teenage skateboarder, what connection did any of this have to Melissa? And, Kate had to admit, even that car could have belonged to someone else. She had no facts. If she went to Roger with a lot of suspicions, wouldn't he just think that she was the one who was jealous and trying to make Melissa look bad? That was too humiliating to contemplate.

A worse thought came to Kate. Even if she had solid proof that Melissa was behind these attacks on her store and reputation, would Roger really be willing to fire her? Somehow she didn't think he would. He seemed so tolerant of her odd behavior that he would probably offer to talk to Melissa about it, but not do anything substantial to correct the situation. Why? He seemed like an efficient manager who wouldn't put up with improper behavior, but when it came to Melissa, he seemed to turn a blind eye. Was that because he loved her? *But then why is he spending Thanksgiving with me rather than with her?* Kate asked herself.

"Here you go," Sarah said, putting the fabric in a bag and handing it to Kate. "And I'll let Jen know what you said. She was so angry at you that she didn't want us to sell you the fabric. 'Let her go to Fabulous Fabrics,' was what she said."

Kate gave a weak smile. "I don't blame her for being angry. In her position I'd have been pretty angry myself."

"Don't worry," Sarah said. "You'll work it out somehow."

"Sure," Kate said confidently. *But how,* she wondered, *exactly how am I going to do that?*

Chapter Ten

Kate backed her van out of the driveway. She'd told Roger that she would drive because she knew the way, but actually it was more because Kate wanted to take him rather than the other way around. She wanted to be in control of the trip. They weren't a couple. He was simply a friend whom she was bringing home for Thanksgiving.

As she drove down the road, Kate realized that it felt good not to be on her way to the shop for a change. She was looking forward to driving north into the mountains of Vermont. Just seeing the farm again, where nothing ever seemed to change, would help her to put her cares and worries behind her, even if only for the day.

If only she could have a place of her own like the farm to retreat to after work. Her mind went back to the house that she had toured yesterday afternoon. The realtor had been an older woman in her fifties. She had clearly liked the house a lot herself, and had eagerly pointed out many of the architectural and decorative details, such as the mahogany pillars outside the opening into what had once been the living room but was now the retail space, and the wide oak flooring in the dining room which had been made into a classroom space. Even the work room was rather nice, having once been a huge butler's pantry with double sinks and several shelves.

The second floor was as large as the first. At some point in time, long before Dagmar had taken over, that floor had been converted into an apartment with a living room, dining room, bathroom, kitchen, and one bedroom. This apartment was separated by a door from the stairway which went up to the third floor. This had also been converted into a sizeable apartment with four large rooms.

"Of course," the realtor had said, "you could always take out the door and combine the second and third floors into one large apartment. That would be big enough for a family."

"There's only me right now," Kate said. "So I'd probably rent out the third floor."

"Well, it's there if you ever need it," the woman replied, giving Kate a sly look, as if to suggest that you never knew when a family would suddenly appear around you.

The realtor had quoted Kate a price that seemed quite reasonable for so much space. Kate's face must have shown her disbelief.

"Even though it's in good condition, it is an old

house. Lots of people are looking for something newer," the woman explained. "Plus this is an area that's zoned for small businesses. That makes it less attractive to couples with families."

As Kate walked out the front door and looked up at the large gray house surrounded by a luxurious green lawn and large trees, she smiled to herself. Working where she lived with no more Jack Martinson coming around hounding her for the rent had a definite appeal, as did just rolling out of bed and coming downstairs to work even in the worst weather. And having her own apartment in a house that she owned— even getting rent from the upstairs rental to supplement what she took in from the shop—all of this looked awfully good.

The realtor stood next to her and also admired the house.

"I'm sure that Dagmar would like another craft store to move in here." The realtor paused. "Both Dagmar and her husband are in Florida now. They're very motivated sellers."

Kate knew that meant that they would be willing to negotiate and take an even lower price for the house. It would certainly be a dream come true.

A dream, that's exactly what it is, Kate told herself, as she turned down the street that Roger had told her he lived on. She still had some money saved from her days at the insurance company, but all of that and more would go into buying out Rhonda. Even if Rhonda agreed to let her spread out the payments over several years, she could only afford a small downpayment on the house. And assuming a bank would accept a small downpayment, how could she meet large mortgage payments every month unless the shop was doing well? Right now Melissa, the queen of Fabulous Fabrics, was doing her best to make that an impossibility. It all seemed pretty hopeless.

Before Kate had a chance to park, Roger came down the steps of one of the townhouse condominiums. He was wearing a leather bomber jacket and tan cords that gave him an adventurous look which was offset only slightly by the fact that he was juggling a pie in each hand. Kate reached over and opened the door so Roger could place the pies on the floor in the back where they would be safe. He looked so good, Kate was glad she'd worn the red turtleneck that she knew accentuated her dark brown hair. She was also glad she'd worn her good tan chinos rather than the ones with fabric paint splatters covering them.

"A pumpkin and a mince. Both traditional favorites," Roger announced as he climbed in beside her.

"You made them yourself?" Kate asked, surprised. She'd never met a man who could do much beyond pushing the start button on the microwave.

"Sure. All you have to do is follow the recipe as long as you know how to find your way around a kitchen. And this place has a pretty good kitchen."

Kate glanced up at the building. "Looks like a nice condo."

"Yeah. I've got a six-month lease from the owner. It's furnished down to the knives and forks."

I really am nuts, Kate thought to herself. *Here I am taking a guy home for Thanksgiving who is my tough-*

*est business competitor, who has a crazy girlfriend,
and who is planning to move on in six months.*

"Do you like all the moving around?" she asked as
they left the parking lot.

"Hate it. I finally get settled down somewhere and
start to feel at home, then another store pops up across
country and off I go."

"The owner of Fabulous Fabrics must have a lot of
confidence in you since he sends you everywhere get
ting new stores started."

Roger nodded. "And I told you about needing the
money to help out my family. But if I had my way,
I'd settle somewhere and put down roots. I'm getting
close to thirty. I don't want to spend my whole life
wandering from fabric store to fabric store."

"I've been thinking about putting down roots myself," Kate said, hoping that didn't sound like too
much of a come-on.

"I thought you already had. Owning your own business is putting down pretty deep roots."

"Well, then, I guess I want my roots to spread out
more," she said, and then went on to tell Roger all
about the house she had looked at.

"That sounds great," Roger said when she paused
to catch her breath. "I'm glad you're taking the idea
of getting into fabric painting seriously. That's one
area where you'll get no competition from the large
chains. You could still sell some of the higher quality
manufactured fabrics and then market your own
painted fabrics as well. You could market by mail order, on the Internet, and through quilt shows."

"And by having the shop right where I live, I

wouldn't have to worry about rent or overhead going up every time I sign a new lease," Kate said.

Roger nodded. "Another plus."

"There's only one problem," Kate said slowly. She had a bad feeling where this was going to lead, but there was no point in making the picture look deceptively rosy to Roger.

"What's that?"

"I might be able to come up with enough money for a small downpayment, but no matter how good a deal I get on the house, I'm going to need to earn enough money each month to pay a sizeable mortgage."

"And when you're starting your own business, it always takes a while before you get much to take home," Roger said. "I imagine the two of you haven't been making much of a profit yet."

Kate nodded. "Hardly anything. Rhonda and I haven't even taken a real salary most months in order to plow as much as possible back into the business. We just pay ourselves enough for rent and food. This was starting to look like the first year when we might actually be able to make a halfway decent living out of the store, but now . . . I'm not so sure."

Roger looked out the window. He stared at the scenery.

"Because of Fabulous Fabrics, you mean?" he finally asked softly.

"That's part of it."

There was also Rhonda deciding to settle down in California with her bronzed Adonis, although Kate wasn't about to tell Roger about that just yet. Then there was crazy Melissa and her campaign of sabotage. Should she tell Roger her suspicions? If he got hostile as a result of hearing her theory, it could make for a long Thanksgiving.

Better to tell him now while we're only twenty minutes from home and can easily return than to wait until we cross the border into Vermont, Kate figured. *If he doesn't like what he hears, I'll just drop him off back home along with his pies. Mom always makes extras anyway.*

Looking straight ahead out the windshield and keeping her voice as even as possible, Kate recounted what the boy across the street had seen the night her store was spray painted. She went on to tell about her order being canceled, and concluded with the story that Sarah at Quilter's Paradise had told her.

When she was finished Roger remained silent. Kate had thought he might immediately respond by saying that she was being silly or jumping to unwarranted conclusions. Even that might have been better than this silence.

"Are you going to say anything?" she finally asked.

"What can I say, Kate? A lot of strange things have been happening to you. I'd be spooked myself if I were in your position. But to blame it all on Melissa seems to me to be going way too far. The only connection to her at all is that boy's claim that he saw a red sports car."

"Do you think he lied?" Kate said sharply.

"I'm not saying that, but almost everyone who buys a sports car probably chooses red. There must be thousands of them around. And the boy didn't even know the make."

"And all the rest of the things that have happened?"

Roger shrugged and turned to look at her. His blue eyes were skeptical.

"Like I said, they are strange events, but it could all be a series of coincidences. Or there could be someone out to get you, but that doesn't mean it has to be Melissa."

"How many enemies do you think I have?" Kate asked.

"Melissa isn't your enemy," Roger replied with a smile that was just patronizing enough to get an angry Kate to tell him about Melissa threatening her in the parking lot at the quilt show.

Roger's face hardened as she told him what had happened. She wasn't sure whether he was angry at her or at Melissa.

"Does that convince you that it's probably Melissa?" Kate asked.

Roger said nothing.

"At least ask her if her car was at my store that night," Kate insisted.

Roger sighed. "It couldn't have been Melissa. We were working together at Fabulous Fabrics when that boy saw her car."

"At eleven o'clock at night?" Kate almost shouted.

She took her eyes off the road for a moment to stare at him. Did he think she was stupid? She'd heard about men who told their wives they were out working with their secretaries at all hours of the night. Was Roger another one like that?

Roger smiled, somehow managing to appear completely innocent. "I know that sounds a bit unbelievable. That's why I didn't mention it at first."

"A bit unbelievable?" Kate said sarcastically.

"But the fact is that Melissa had made some major mistakes on our last inventory, and I wouldn't let her leave until we got it all straightened out. We were there until midnight, and trust me, I know exactly how long it took there because Melissa was continually reminding me of the time in a very loud voice."

Kate smiled in spite of herself. That certainly sounded like Melissa.

"So you see," Roger went on, "you really don't have any evidence that Melissa is the person doing these things to you."

"Maybe not, but I do know that she threatened me. She claimed that you were hers and bad things would happen to me if I so much as looked in your direction."

Roger grinned. "I can see that you weren't very impressed or you wouldn't be here now."

"I'm beginning to have second thoughts," Kate replied.

He reached over and gave her shoulder a squeeze.

"Please don't. I can assure you that Melissa and I do not have any kind of personal relationship."

Kate was tempted to make him raise his hand and swear it under oath.

"Well, you may not think you have a relationship with her, but she certainly wants to have one with you."

"Look, this is going to sound conceited, but there's

only one way to put it: Melissa has a terrible crush on me. She's been spoiled from childhood by rich parents, and she expects to get everything she wants. But you have to believe me, any romantic relationship is strictly in her mind."

"Nonetheless, you've got to do something about it. Why don't you fire her?"

Roger snorted. "Oh, that would look good. Boss fires his female employee because she has a crush on him. There's nothing Melissa would like better than to get a couple of high-priced lawyers handling that one."

"Would she do that?"

"Of course. Remember she was ready to sue you over that little advertisement. She'd figure that if she sued, maybe she could blackmail me into getting involved with her."

"You can't force someone to love you," Kate said.

"Maybe in Melissa's twisted world you can."

Kate watched the trees and fields speed past as she absorbed the grim truth of what Roger had said. Somehow the country seemed so peaceful compared to the world of people. But from living on the farm, she knew that nature could be as harsh as any human reality.

"I don't have a solution for you, Roger, but I do know that you can't go on working with Melissa. That's only feeding her fantasy. Somehow you have to get separated from her."

"I can't fire her. And if I quit, how will I help my family?" he asked.

"Couldn't you talk to the owner of Fabulous Fabrics? He thinks a lot of you. Maybe he'd transfer Melissa somewhere far away."

"That's an idea," he said.

When Kate looked over, his eyes slid away from hers as though he didn't want her to see that the idea was impossible.

Why couldn't he do that? Kate wondered. Was there a good reason or did he, perhaps, like having a beautiful, infatuated young woman orbiting around him? What man wouldn't find that appealing to his vanity? But Kate knew the danger of the situation because, as long as Melissa was in Roger's vicinity, it would only take one moment of weakness on his part and Melissa would have him in her clutches by fair means or foul.

Chapter Eleven

"Katie," her mother said softly, but with an undertone of deep happiness. She opened her arms wide and hugged her daughter. "And this must be Roger," she said, reaching out to shake his hand.

Roger gave one of the pies to Kate so he could grasp her mother's hand. "Nice to meet you, Mrs. Manning."

"Call me Dora. No need to stand on formalities."

They went down the hall and into the living room which was on the right. A lean, rugged man in his mid-fifties got out of the rocker by the fire and walked over to them.

"You remember Harry Smyth. He owns the next farm over the hill. He's going to be having Thanksgiving with us this year."

Roger and Kate shook hands with the man, who smiled and said how pleased he was to see Kate after a number of years. Kate glanced quizzically at her mother.

"Why don't you sit in there with Harry?" Kate's mother said to Roger. "Katie and I will go into the kitchen and put these fine pies in the refrigerator."

The two women went into the large kitchen that filled one corner of the back of the house. Kate's mother carefully placed the pies in the refrigerator, taking much more time than was necessary, while Kate hovered nearby.

Finally, her mother stood up straight and turned to look Kate in the eye.

"I suppose you have a question for me."

"Why is Mr. Smyth here? I thought we always had Thanksgiving together, just the two of us."

The words came out louder than she expected, and her mother winced. She moved into the corner of the kitchen farthest from the living room before answering.

"I'm sure you remember that I told you Harry's wife, Rachel, died right after Christmas last year."

"Sure. She was one of your best friends. I remember your telling me that she had passed away."

"Well, I'd see Harry at church every week. And we'd talk about this and that. After all, we'd been friends for over twenty years. Once in a while I'd bring him over a casserole, although the man is so independent he hardly needs a woman to cook for him. I see Roger must be the same way by the look of those pies."

"Let's stay on the point, Mom. You were telling me how you were fattening up Harry."

Her mother frowned. "Some nights he'd ask me to stay for dinner and share the casserole with him. We'd sit and talk about our farms and our children."

She paused and Kate was surprised to see her mother's eyes fill with tears.

"And I realized how long it's been since I've done anything like that—just sat there like that with a man and talked." She dabbed at her eyes with a large white handkerchief she pulled out of her apron pocket.

"I didn't know you were lonely, Mom. You can always come to visit Rhonda and me," Kate said hoarsely.

"It's not that I'm lonely exactly. And I dearly love visiting you, Katie, but it isn't the same. What I'm trying to tell you is that Harry and I are . . . seeing each other."

"Seeing each other?" Kate asked faintly.

"And we're planning to get married."

"Married! When?"

"Soon. We haven't quite worked out all the details."

Kate sank down on one of the wooden kitchen chairs. Her mother bent over her and put her arms around Kate's shoulders.

"Your father's been dead for over ten years, Katie. No one will ever replace him in my memory or my affections, but I don't want to spend the rest of my life drying up like some old apple that's fallen out of the bushel basket."

Kate managed to smile at her mother's choice of words. "I know what you're saying makes sense. It's just a shock."

"I know. I'm sorry to break it to you this way, but

I didn't want to let you know over the phone. And to tell you the truth, things between Harry and me have been moving along a bit faster than I expected the last few weeks. I decided that I'd better take this occasion to tell you now, face to face."

Kate squeezed her mother's hand. "Well, I'm happy for you, Mom. For both of you."

"There something else you should know."

Kate sighed. What next?

"You'd better tell me quick. Am I going to be getting a little half-brother or -sister?" Kate asked, half-joking. Today anything seemed possible.

Her mother laughed. "No fear of that. It's about the farm. You know how the only income for years has been from the twenty acres of grazing pasture we rent out to the dairy farm and from the sale of apples from the orchard in the fall."

Kate nodded.

"It's always been enough to make ends meet as long as I lived a simple life. Your father's life insurance paid your way through college and gave me a bit of a cushion, but as I've gotten older, I've been thinking more and more about needing a little nest egg to support me in my old age."

"You know you could always come live with me," Kate blurted out.

"That might not always be your choice alone," her mother said, casting a meaningful look toward the living room.

Kate sat up stiffly in the chair. "Any husband of mine would want me to take care of my mother."

"Maybe so, but perhaps I don't want to be taken

care of, at least not if I can help it. And remember, I won't be alone now, I'll have Harry. But anyway, it isn't a problem any more."

"Why not?"

"A company called Apex Systems has offered to buy the farm from me."

"Who are they?" Kate gasped. First, her mother decides to get married, and now the farm is being sold as well. She took a deep breath to clear her head. And she had thought she was coming home to a place where nothing ever changed.

"Something to do with computers. They're from around Boston. The man from the company said that they don't need to be near a city any more, what with the Internet and all. Southern Vermont was just the location they were looking for to put up their new building."

"I don't believe it," Kate mumbled.

"Neither did I at first. But I got a good lawyer down in Burlington. He looked over the whole deal and said it was for real." A sly smile stole over her mother's face. "They're paying me over a million and a half dollars for the land."

"Really? Are you sure?"

Her mother nodded, and her face broke into a huge grin. "Can you imagine that, Katie? After all these years trying to get by on the farm, worrying about whether the furnace would last another year or if the truck's transmission was making a strange sound, to suddenly not have all those problems to think about. I feel like I've gotten a new lease on life."

"I've always admired how you handled those problems, Mom. You always told me that I should learn to deal with whatever came along."

Her mother nodded. "And so you should. I hope that I've brought you up to be strong and to be able to face whatever the world dishes out. But life includes the good as well as the bad, Katie. I never meant to teach you that suffering was a worthwhile thing in itself. When good fortune comes along, you should sit back and enjoy it."

Kate felt the tears begin to flow down her cheeks. "I am happy for you, Mom. This is wonderful news."

As they hugged her mother said, "I'm only sorry that the farm will be torn down. I know this is where you grew up, and it must mean a lot to you."

"It does. But I think maybe I've come on a substitute."

Kate told her mother about the house she'd been looking at. That led to her pouring out the whole story about Rhonda's wedding plans, and the problems she had been having with Melissa and the store.

When she was done her mother shook her head.

"Good grief, Katie, if I heard that on a soap opera I wouldn't believe it. I have to say that, as much as I love Rhonda, she's never seemed to have much of a head for business. I know that you'll miss her as a friend, but Golden Needles might be better off without her."

"I suppose," Kate said doubtfully.

"And you go make an offer on that house of yours. By the first of next month I'll easily be able to give you enough money so that you'll be able to buy it without a mortgage plus give Rhonda the money for her share of the business."

"But that's your money." Kate paused. "Yours and Harry's."

"No. Harry and I have decided to keep our finances separate. He has three children, and we don't want either of our families getting resentful because we've remarried. I'm not saying that I won't use my money to see that Harry and I have a good life, but all my assets will remain in my name. When I die . . ."

Kate reached out and touched her mother's arm.

"Don't worry, Kate," her mother said laughing, "I expect to go on for another forty years now that I've got Harry. But when that time comes, all that I have will go to you. So there's no reason why you shouldn't have a little in advance."

"No. You always taught me to make my own way. But I will take the money from you as a loan. And I'll pay some of it back to you every month."

Her mother looked a little hurt, but then she smiled. "I guess I did raise you to be pretty independent after all. If that's the way you want it, then that's the way it will be. An interest-free loan is still a lot better than what you'll get from the bank."

"Great! That solves all my problems."

"Not quite. This girl, Melissa, is another story," her mother said soberly. "You and Roger are going to have to work this out."

Kate felt the whole world of reality come crashing down around her again. Here was a problem that money wasn't going to solve.

"Maybe I should just forget the whole thing—never

see Roger again and hope that Melissa stops trying to sabotage me."

"You don't mean that," her mother said softly.

Kate smiled. "No, I guess I don't."

"Are you sure Roger isn't right and that she might not be the one doing these things?"

"You didn't see the expression on her face when she told me to stay away from him. I'm certain she's behind it all."

Her mother frowned and studied the green tile floor.

"How do you feel about Roger?" she asked.

"I . . . I'm not sure. I sort of like him, but we haven't really had much of a chance to get to know each other under normal circumstances."

"I wonder if you're being completely honest with yourself," her mother said.

"What do you mean?"

"You've been threatened by this woman, your shop was spray painted, your order was short circuited, and she's been spreading stories about you. And yet you're still seeing Roger. That should tell you that whatever you feel about Roger, it's a lot stronger than just 'sort of' liking him."

Harry stepped into the kitchen. "Everything all right in here, ladies?" he asked a bit anxiously.

"No problem, hon," Kate's mother answered. "We were just talking about things. We'll be right out."

Kate gave Harry the brightest smile she could muster to show that she accepted his relationship with her mother. Harry gave her a relieved smile in return.

"Don't rush," Harry replied. "Roger and I are having a fine time talking about fishing."

Fishing, Kate thought, *that just shows how little I know about Roger. There's something we have in common.* Her father had loved to fish and had taught her.

"We'll be right out," Kate's mother said.

When Harry went back into the living room, Kate's mother looked her in the eye.

"If you feel as strongly about Roger as I think you do, you have to find some way out of this problem with Melissa. And if Roger cares about you, he'll be willing to do his share too."

"But somehow I get the feeling that he isn't willing to risk offending Melissa. That makes me wonder whether he cares for her in some way even though he says that he doesn't."

Her mother shook her head. "Sitting around speculating isn't going to solve your problem, Katie. Be honest with him and expect him to be honest with you. If he's the type of man that you'd want to spend your life with, he'll tell you the truth once he knows that you really care about him."

"How do I prove that to him?" Kate asked.

Her mother smiled. "That's easy. That's the part that comes naturally."

Her mother got up and headed for the door into the dining room.

"Mom?" Kate asked, not moving from her chair.

Her mother turned back to her.

"What is it that you see in Harry? I mean what about him told you that he was the one for you?"

"The same thing I saw in your father," her mother replied with a sad smile. "He's reliable and honest, but underneath all that serious manly exterior, he's really a boy with a tremendous sense of fun."

She opened the door and led Kate into the living room. Roger and Harry were engrossed in a discussion about tying lures. Both stopped immediately when the women entered the room. Harry looked up at Dora with anticipation, while Roger's concerned expression showed that he had sensed the tension in the air. Kate gave him a smile to indicate that everything was okay. He quickly smiled back.

Her mother took a bottle of champagne out of an ice bucket by the side of the sofa.

"Harry, would you open this?" she said. "I believe we have something to celebrate."

Chapter Twelve

As they sat down for Thanksgiving dinner, Kate became aware that the large, simple room was more decorated than she could remember it ever being. Her mother had purchased a dramatic floral centerpiece, and a display of gourds harvested from Harry's farm was on the sideboard. Candles flickered on either end of the table, and Kate's mother gave her a conspiratorial wink as she drew the drapes and switched off the overhead light to provide the room with a romantic atmosphere.

"Can't see what I've got on my plate," Harry said in a teasing voice as the turkey and all the trimmings were passed around.

"We'll have to go by feel," Roger chimed in with a show of male unity.

Kate couldn't believe how quickly Roger and Harry had started acting like old friends. Nothing like fishing to bring men together. Although the conversation turned a bit formal as her mother asked Roger about himself, his answers were so unforced and natural that soon everyone relaxed. Before long Harry was joking about how he had never expected to marry a million-airess and how Kate's mother was threatening to turn Harry's simple farm home into a Hollywood mansion, complete with hot tub.

It's always seemed so wonderful to me to have Thanksgiving here alone with my mother, Kate thought, as she watched the candlelight dance off the walls. *A time to share memories and confidences. But somehow this Thanksgiving is richer for having other people to share it with. It's filled with new possibilities for the future rather than with remembrances of the past.*

She looked at Roger talking to her mother. His an-imated features showed that he was enjoying himself. When he glanced over at her a few moments later and winked, she felt for one giddy moment that no matter what problems they faced, they wouldn't prove insur-mountable as long as she and Roger faced them to-gether.

After dinner Harry quickly offered to help clean up. Kate and Roger joined him, but Kate's mother sug-gested that they might like to take a walk around the farm before heading back home. Roger put on his leather jacket and helped Kate into her fleece coat. She studied him as he walked ahead of her to open the door. He really was handsome—not in the cute, almost pretty way of Nick, but in a sort of rugged, unpolished way. Odd, now that she considered it, how he was rather like a younger version of Harry.

He caught her looking at him and his eyes seemed to read her thoughts. Kate gave an embarrassed grin and went out the door onto the country porch.

"So where shall we walk?" he asked, gazing around him at the barn and surrounding pastures.

"Up the hill," Kate said, pointing to the small knoll that rose to the left of the farmhouse. It ended in a small clump of trees at the top. "I always used to sit up there when I was a girl and had a lot to think about."

As they walked up the hill, Kate informed Roger about Rhonda's plans to stay in California. She also told him about her mother's offer to loan her the money for the house. Be honest, Mom had said, and expect him to be honest in return. *I hope it works,* Kate thought.

"That's wonderful, Kate," Roger said. "It seems like everything is working out. You'll have a place to live and do your fabric painting, and Fabulous Fabrics won't be your direct competitor any more." He grinned. "We can stop being friendly enemies."

He took her hand in his as he said this. The sky was iron gray and it was cold enough for Kate to appreciate the warmth of his hand around hers. But she knew that she had a painful question to ask. She only hoped that they'd go down the hill still holding hands.

When they arrived at the top, they stood for a moment appreciating the view. Fields spread out in the foreground as far as the eye could see, punctuated occasionally by small stands of trees. In the distance were the mountains, green in the summer, but now barren of leaves, separating valley from valley.

"Let's sit over there," Kate said, pointing to a fallen log. "That's my usual spot."

They sat and looked down on the farm for a few minutes without speaking. Roger put his arm around her.

"Are you sad because all of this is going to disappear?"

Kate shook her head. "Not really. When I was a little girl, I'd look at those mountains and think that the whole world was out there somewhere on the other side waiting for me. The last place I wanted to be was here, cut off from everything. But for the past few years, I've sat here and thought that they were actually my friends, protecting me from all the ugly and difficult things that the world threw at me. This was my safe little haven where I could hide from what was painful or bad. A few times I've even thought of moving back here and living with Mom, maybe getting a job down in Brattleboro just to make ends meet and coming back to stay on the farm."

"You don't feel that way now?"

"I think that would be giving up." Kate laughed shortly. "I also think I'd be bored out of my mind in a month. No, it was just that Golden Needles was a strain and Rhonda really wasn't all that much help. And there were other problems. Anyway, I had no one in my life to share things with, the good or the bad."

Roger reached over and turned her face toward his. Slowly he kissed her. Kate felt the softness of his lips and for a moment nothing else existed. He pulled her close and she relaxed into his arms. His hands gently kneaded her neck and shoulders as she snuggled deeper into his chest, smelling the pungent leather of his coat.

"Do you think you could share those things with me?" Roger asked after a moment.

Kate slid out from under his arm and turned to look at him.

"There's something we have to talk about first."

"Okay. Shoot. You ask and I'll answer," he replied with a grin.

"This is serious."

Roger's expression turned somber.

"It's about Melissa."

Roger glanced away with an expression of disgust. "Do we have to talk about her right now? Every time we get a chance to be alone she comes between us, either physically or in spirit."

Kate took his hand. "I want you to be completely honest with me."

"Don't you think I have been?"

"Not completely."

Roger opened his mouth to protest, then closed it again.

"You said earlier that you'd never had a relationship with Melissa, but that she had a crush on you. When I suggested that you talk to the owner of Fabulous Fabrics about changing the arrangement, you brushed me off. I want to know why."

Roger looked into the distance for a long time. So long that Kate began to worry that perhaps he'd lied about having a relationship with Melissa. How would she feel if he confessed to having been involved with the Dragon Woman? Would that be enough to completely change her feelings toward Roger? Could a man who loved a virtual lunatic be trusted to form a stable relationship? Was he stable himself?

Finally, he turned toward her. "I'm going to tell you the whole story, but you have to promise that you won't repeat it. I'm breaking a promise by telling you this."

"I won't tell anyone," Kate said.

Roger sighed. "The man who owns the entire Fabulous Fabrics chain is Melissa's father, Stanford Harper."

"I thought you said Melissa's name was Hardgrove."

"That was part of the deception. He didn't want anyone in the store to know that Melissa was his daughter. He made me swear to keep it a secret."

"I'm sorry. I don't understand."

"It's a long story. Melissa is Stan's only child, and from what I've heard, she'd been in trouble all her life. She was in and out of expensive prep schools as a child and dropped out of more colleges than most folks have heard of as an adult."

"If they sent her away all the time, maybe that's as much her parents' fault as hers," Kate said, almost feeling sorry for Melissa.

"Could be," Roger admitted. "Stan isn't the easiest guy in the world to get along with, and his wife has a reputation for being an alcoholic. Their usual way of dealing with Melissa was to keep her as far away as possible for as long as possible."

"Is that how she ended up here?"

"Sort of. I was at Stan's house for a meeting. It just happened to be one of those rare times when Melissa was staying at home. We met and talked for a few moments, nothing out of the ordinary. A few days later Stan calls and says that he wants me to open a new store in Massachusetts and to take on Melissa as my assistant."

"Does she have any experience with fabrics?" Kate asked.

"Only what she's learned by buying expensive clothes her whole life." Roger paused and ran a hand over his face. "Okay, to be fair, she does have good taste. You've seen how she dresses. She has a sense of fashion. Some women could spend as much as she does and still not look half as good."

Kate felt a twinge of jealousy and was ashamed of herself. Roger had said nothing that wasn't true. She'd just been childishly hoping that he'd never noticed how attractive Melissa was.

"Anyway," Roger continued, "Stan made it clear to me that I was responsible for his daughter's rehabilitation. He also gave me some not-so-subtle hints that Melissa liked me, and he wouldn't mind having me for a son-in-law if things worked out that way."

The expression on Roger's face was one of extreme distress, as though someone had just recommended that he have a root canal without anaethesia. Kate almost laughed in relief.

"I take it that you aren't considering joining the Fabulous Fabrics family," Kate teased.

"Easy for you to laugh. Melissa has no interest in

doing her job. All she does is strut around the store criticizing the employees for their appearance or accusing them of not respecting her authority. And who can blame them? They don't know she's Stan's daughter. They think she's some stuck-up witch that I hired."

Kate nodded her sympathy.

"All she does most of the time is warn me that I'd better be nice to her or she'll tell Daddy that I'm not helping her to learn the business. The only thing that's saved me so far is that I've been gentle with her and made excuses for why we can't go out together. I keep telling her it wouldn't look good to the other employees if we got involved."

"Sounds like you're being 'pursued' by the boss's daughter."

"I guess I am," Roger said with a bitter laugh. "Now I know what women have had to put up with over the years. Talk about role reversal. It would be funny if it weren't such a problem."

Kate smiled. "You can handle an ugly drunk but not Melissa."

"She's far worse than any lush with a bad attitude."

"So what are you going to do about her?" Kate asked.

Roger shook his head. "I'd hate to lose my job, but I don't think I can go on much longer this way. Melissa is putting more and more pressure on me since you've been on the scene."

"Not to mention putting pressure on me."

"If you're right about what's been happening."

"You're still not convinced?" Kate asked, exasperated.

"Oh, Melissa is up to doing something like that, but as I told you on the ride up, she couldn't have been there the night your shop got sprayed. And you said that she wasn't the woman who was spreading the rumors about you in the quilt store."

"Okay. But you've still got to get away from her somehow," Kate insisted.

"I know. I'm just not sure how."

As they walked down the hill, Kate took Roger's hand. He looked over at her, his brow still furrowed with concern.

"Don't worry," Kate said. "Things will work out."

Roger shook his head. "Not by themselves. You have to work them out yourself."

Reluctantly, Kate had to agree.

Chapter Thirteen

The red numbers on the alarm clock showed that it was one o'clock. Kate flopped back in the bed and sighed. She had tossed and turned for hours. She had to get some sleep, she repeated to herself like a mantra. Back in the fall, she and Rhonda foolishly had set up a class for the day after Thanksgiving and a surprising large number of people had signed up. It was a class on making a quilted Christmas tree with an oriental flavor. Kate figured the students were women who didn't go away for Thanksgiving and dreaded the thought of spending all of the long weekend hanging around at home with the husband and kids while trying to decide what to do with leftover turkey. It was a class scheduled to begin at nine, so she really needed to get some sleep.

What was keeping her awake wasn't all bad. The memory of the lingering kisses in the car in front of

Roger's condo upon their return from the farm were hardly what she would call unpleasant. The recollection of his strong hands and gentle touch made her smile to herself in the darkness. Roger had invited her in, but she had suggested that they wait for another time. The specter of Melissa still hung over them, and Kate didn't want their romance to begin in the shadow of another woman.

Another thing that was keeping her awake was the anticipation of being able to call the realtor tomorrow and proceed with buying the house. Upon leaving the farm, her mother had given her a generous check she could use to start the process. The closing on the farm was coming at the end of January, so Kate could conclude her purchase of her house any time after that. Visions of how she would set up her shop and decorate the upstairs apartment floated throughout her mind, mixed in with images of Roger. Although she tried to reign in her imagination, she pictured the two of them living together in the cozy second floor apartment.

Her mind finally raced itself to exhaustion. It seemed to Kate that she had just fallen asleep when the alarm began ringing. It took her a second to realize that it was the telephone. She fumbled the receiver into her hand, at the same time noticing that the clock was just going on five.

"Hello." If this was a crank call, she was definitely going to reach for her police whistle.

"Kate, this is Jack Martinson."

She was instantly awake.

"What's up, Jack?"

"There's been a fire."

The picture of her store blazing upward into the night sky filled Kate's mind.

"It's a fire in the dumpster behind your shop," he went on. "It could have reached your shop except somebody called the fire department."

"So it didn't reach the shop, right, Jack?" Kate asked quickly, wanting some firm reassurance.

"No. But this isn't good for the mall, Kate."

A few choice words about Jack's precious mall ran through Kate's head.

"I'm coming down there," Kate said.

"That's not really necessary," Jack said, switching directions. "The fire is just about out. There's really nothing to see. The flames didn't even scorch the back wall. It was just a garbage fire. Some kid probably threw a match in the dumpster to see what would happen. Probably one of those skateboarders."

"Okay, Jack. I'll be in by nine and look things over," Kate said, cutting him off before he could go on about his favorite topic. Discussing skateboarders starting fires at five in the morning, that was a stretch even for Jack.

She lay back down and stared into the darkness. Was this the hand of Melissa reaching out once again to wreak havoc? As usual there was no proof. Kate stayed there for a few minutes trying to decide whether it was worthwhile attempting to go back to sleep. Finally she figured that it would be better to get up and continue hand quilting the quilt she planned to enter in the Christmas Day show. She only had three weeks, and about a third of the squares remained to be finished.

Kate put on her robe and made herself a cup of coffee. She sat on the sofa with her legs curled under her and began the slow process of making the rows of tiny stitches. Although each stitch was small, together they helped secure the quilt and ensured that the fabric would hold together evenly. At the same time, they also gave an overall depth and dimension to the pattern.

An older woman had once told Kate that she thought of each quilting stitch as being a small life experience. Just as the tiny tight stitches were what gave meaning to the larger whole, so the small experiences of life were what gave a person's entire existence its form and texture.

Double wedding ring. That was the pattern Kate had chosen months ago. Had her unconscious mind been telling her something, Kate wondered? Had the time come for her to make the kind of commitment that she had avoided since her days with Nick? She didn't have an answer to these questions, but as her hands moved swiftly and surely, embedding the neat rows of stitches, she found that her mind had reached a place where finding answers didn't matter.

"You see, Kate," Jack Martinson said urgently, pointing at a scorched dumpster that only a blind person wouldn't be able to see. "That's what we have to put up with today. And the police . . . the police . . . all they do is smile and say that kind of thing happens. Just be happy there wasn't any damage."

Kate nodded impatiently. She had six women in the

shop cutting strips of fabric and didn't want to leave them without guidance for long.

"I guess the police are right," she said. "We have to be happy that it wasn't worse."

Jack's scowl showed that he wasn't going to be so easily reconciled. "Probably the carting service is going to hold me responsible for this. Who knows what one of those dumpster things costs?"

"It doesn't seem to be badly damaged," Kate said. "Anyway, won't insurance cover it?"

"Oh, sure. Just like insurance covered the damage to the front of your shop. If I put in a claim to cover the cleaning expenses for that graffiti, my rates are going to shoot through the roof. I'm almost losing money on this place already."

Not wanting to hear any more about Jack's financial woes, Kate opened the back door to the shop.

"Well, I'd better be getting back."

"Just a minute, Kate," Jack said, suddenly sounding more focused.

She turned back and saw that a shrewd expression had replaced his usual appearance of untempered anxiety.

"I want to know the truth, Kate. Has someone started some kind of vendetta against you? Spray painting your shop and now this. Somehow it doesn't feel like a few skateboarders to me. Is there something more serious going on?"

"Not that I know of," Kate said, hoping that the vagueness of her statement avoided a lie. There was, after all, a world of difference between suspecting and knowing.

Jack squinted at her suspiciously. "Your lease runs out at the end of February."

As if you didn't tell me every other week, Kate thought.

"I've been thinking about it. And I don't believe that the larger shop I plan to make by combining your space with Prehistoric Platters would really be right for you."

He stared at Kate. She wondered if he expected her to plead to be allowed to stay in his pathetic mall and if he was then planning to follow up with some huge rent increase. She would be leaving happily at the end of her lease if the house deal went through, but Kate wasn't going to give Jack the satisfaction of knowing that.

She shrugged. "You do whatever you have to do, Jack. But did you ever consider that if someone is purposely vandalizing my store, they might not be out to get me but rather out to get you? We all have enemies."

Kate went back into her shop leaving Jack looking more worried than ever.

Three hours later when her students made a beeline down the mall to the luncheonette to grab something to eat, Kate called Fabulous Fabrics. Making her way via phone through several layers of employees, she finally reached Roger.

"This is an unexpected pleasure. I thought you had sworn an oath never to call the number of Fabulous Fabrics," Roger joked.

"Always keep a close watch on the enemy, that's

my motto. What cut-rate goods are you flogging to-day?"

"Good thing Melissa can't hear you say that. She'd be notifying the Supreme Court."

"Speaking of Melissa," Kate began.

"Do we have to?"

"Do you happen to know where she was yester-day?"

"What's happened now?" Roger asked anxiously.

Kate told him about the fire in the dumpster.

"Well, I hate to burst your bubble, but she couldn't have done this either."

"Why not?"

"Surprisingly enough, she actually went home for Thanksgiving."

"I thought she never went home," Kate said.

"For some reason this time she did. She was kind of secretive about it."

"Are you sure that she actually went?"

Roger sighed. "I took her to the airport before you picked me up yesterday and put her on the plane my-self. I even waited to watch it take off. It was a direct flight to Denver where her folks live."

Kate frowned at the phone. "Are you sure she's still there?"

"She was when I called two hours ago."

"You called her?" Kate asked, some of her insecu-rity about Roger and Melissa returning.

"I called her father. And I have some good news on the Melissa front. I was thinking about our conversa-tion yesterday and what you said about my having to get her separated from me. So I called her father and suggested that he send her on a tour of the stores in the west for the next couple of weeks. I told him it would be a good way to broaden her base of experience. He took to the idea. I'm hoping that maybe she'll run into a store manager out there that she likes better than me."

"Will Melissa go along with that?" Kate asked. Somehow this sounded too good to be true.

"If Stan sweetens it with a car and a new wardrobe, he thinks she might go along with it."

Poor Melissa, Kate found herself thinking. No wonder she was a mess.

"Can we get together tonight?" Roger asked. "I'll be off at six. How about we go out for dinner?"

"You can pick me up at the store if we aren't going anywhere very fancy." She looked down at her green sweater and tan skirt. She was dressed a bit better than usual. All she'd need to do was brush off the loose threads from being around so much sewing.

"A woman who doesn't want to go somewhere fancy. I knew you were the one for me," Roger said.

"Wait until I move into my new place where I can run right upstairs and change. Then you'll be singing a different tune."

After Kate hung up the phone, she sat staring at the counter top thinking about how sad Melissa's life must be. Then she heard the bell over the door ring.

Tim, wearing a sweatshirt and oversized pants, came into the shop carrying his skateboard.

"No school today, so you're getting an early start on the skateboarding?" Kate asked.

Tim made a face. "This place is getting to be no

good. Even the guy down there who owns the luncheonette is hassling us, saying we're bad for business."

"That fire last night didn't help," said Kate.

"You don't think that was me?" he asked in a hurt
tone.

"Of course not."

Tim stepped nearer the counter and spoke in a low
voice even though no one else was in the shop.

"I saw what happened."

"You did?"

"Well, kinda. I was asleep, you know, but this noise
woke me up. Like a metal door banging. Whoever it
was must have let go of the lid on the dumpster as
they were opening it, and it hit the side. So I got up
and looked out the window."

He paused for effect.

"What did you see?" Kate asked.

"It was that same red car. This time it was parked
near the end of the mall. I got out of bed to go see
who it was."

"Tim, I told you that you should tell your parents
and let them call the police."

"Yeah. Well, anyway, by the time I got dressed and
out the door, the car was racing off up the street. I
went over to look anyway, just to see if there were
any clues. That's when I saw the fire and called the
fire department. I didn't tell them who I was."

"You should have given your name. You were a
hero."

Tim looked at her as if she were stupid. "They'd
probably blame me for starting the fire so I could call
it in and look good. Better off I stay out of it."

Kate decided he was probably right.

"Well, thank you, Tim. What you did may have saved my shop."

The boy smiled shyly as though he wasn't accustomed to being praised. He stared at the quilts that were hanging on every available wall space.

"Did you make that?" Tim said, eyeing a quilted wall hanging of tropical fish that was behind the counter.

"Yes."

"That's neat."

Kate reached up and took it off the wall. She rolled it up and handed it to the surprised boy.

"It's yours."

"Mine?"

"It's the least I can do to thank you for saving my shop."

His eyes widened and he took the gift. "I'll hang it on my wall in my bedroom. This stuff you make is really great."

"Any time you want to come back and look around, be my guest," Kate said.

The boy nodded as he left the store holding his quilt in one hand and his skateboard in the other.

Kate smiled at the picture, then her smile turned to a frown. If Roger was right, it couldn't have been Melissa who had torched her dumpster. But then who could it be? She'd told Jack that we all have enemies. Maybe she should have added that we all have more than one.

Chapter Fourteen

They went to Diavolo's, a very nice northern Italian restaurant in an old mansion on the outskirts of town that was fancier than Kate had expected. She was relieved to find that, although not the most fashionably dressed woman there, her outfit wasn't an embarrassment. They were seated in an intimate alcove off the main room. Kate suspected the location had been a special request of Roger's. It made her feel as though they were all by themselves and could concentrate solely on each other.

"Here's to many, many more evenings just like this one," Roger said, holding up his glass.

Kate touched her glass to his and looked into his blue eyes, as he stared directly into hers. The candlelight played over his rugged features, casting shadows which suggested that here was a complicated man a woman could know for a long time without ever completely understanding. But it might be fun to make the effort, Kate thought to herself as she put the glass to her lips.

She reached across the table and playfully tapped the back of his hand.

"I thought you weren't going to take me anywhere fancy. I might have been underdressed."

He smiled. "No matter what you were wearing, you'd be the most glamorous woman here."

"I can see I'm going to have to be careful around you. You really know how to sweet-talk a woman."

"It's not sweet talk when you think it's true," he replied.

Kate broke eye contact. "You really are dangerous," she said, smiling despite herself.

"Nope. I'm just giddy with excitement at the idea that we can finally start seeing each other without worrying about Melissa interrupting us. This last month has been one of those bad dreams where you keep running, trying for something that keeps receding just out of reach." He paused for a moment. "What I've been trying to reach is you."

Kate sighed. "I hope you're right and things are finally going to work for us."

"Kate," a man's voice said. As Kate looked up, the man bent down and kissed her firmly on the lips.

She pulled her head back in surprise and stared at the figure standing over her. Roger began to stand.

"Has it been that long Kate?" the man asked, brushing the comma of hair back from his forehead. "Don't you recognize me?"

"Nick?" Kate gasped.

"Do I look so different?" he asked, grinning boyishly.

"No. Well . . . I guess you do, actually."

It wasn't that his physical appearance was so different. He was still strikingly handsome with deep brown eyes and wavy hair. But Kate had to admit that she'd never seen him so well dressed. The European cut suit—splendid material, Kate noted professionally—emphasized his lithe, slender body. It looked as if the guy she'd seen lounging mostly in cutoffs and T-shirts had suddenly become a professional. Even his stance, balanced evenly on both feet with his head erect, indicated a new attitude. Gone was the look of casual indifference, replaced by a bearing that seemed to proclaim that here was a man with focus and a sense of purpose.

She heard Roger clear his throat.

"Nick this is my friend, Roger Garrison. Roger, this is Nick Laughton."

The men shook hands tentatively the way boxers do before a fight.

"Nick has been living on the west coast for . . . how long is it now Nick?"

She knew that it would be exactly two years on Christmas Eve, the night that he had decided to go find himself instead of marrying her, but Kate wasn't going to give him the satisfaction of showing that she had kept track.

"Two years," Nick said, smiling knowingly at her as if to say that he saw through her deception. "I just got back yesterday."

"What were you doing on the west coast?" Roger asked in an overly polite tone.

"I finished up my law degree," Nick said. He turned his attention to Kate. "Finally, I got things together and found out what really mattered to me. Took me long enough."

"Why did you come back?" Kate asked. Her serious tone of voice made the casual question hang in the air as though a lot depended on it.

Nick glanced at Roger. "Well, I decided that I wanted to practice law in Massachusetts, so I've come back to take the bar exam." He paused for a moment, then turned to Kate. "Among other things."

Kate felt herself blush.

"Well, I'd better get back to my table," Nick said, gesturing across the room to a table where several people were settling into their seats. Kate recognized Nick's mother and sisters. They waved across the room as if delighted to see her.

"I guess I'll run into you around town," Kate said.

"You certainly will," Nick replied, giving Roger a quick nod as he walked back across the room.

"An old friend?" Roger asked dryly.

Kate toyed with her fork and nodded.

"Now he's a lawyer," Roger said.

"Looks like it," Kate replied, relieved to see that their food was arriving.

"He seemed pretty happy to see you."

"I guess," Kate said.

"I know," Roger said.

The dinner was spoiled. Although Kate knew the food looked fabulous and must taste the same, she could hardly focus on what she was putting into her mouth, while Roger chewed each piece with the grim thoroughness of someone determined to get through a painful experience. They answered each other's questions briefly, distracted by the laughter from the table on the other side of the room where Nick's light-hearted banter seemed to be contagious.

When they had barely done justice to the meal, they agreed to skip coffee and dessert. They walked in silence across the parking lot to Roger's car. The trip back to Golden Needles was mercifully short.

They sat silently in front of the shop for a moment. Kate had the feeling that if she got out of the car now without speaking she'd never see Roger again.

"This is a small town, Roger, and I've lived here for five years. We're bound to run into people that I've gone out with on occasion."

"I understand that. But this Nick was a bit more than that, wasn't he?"

"We were engaged once, but now it's over."

"I see."

She turned to look at him. His face seemed frozen in the lights of the dashboard.

"What's the matter?" she asked.

"I saw the way he looked at you. He loves you, Kate."

"Oh, that's just Nick. He always did have a good line."

Roger turned to look at her. "I don't think so."

Kate didn't bother to deny it again.

"And I'll tell you something else. By the way you

were looking at him, I think that maybe you feel the same way."

Kate paused. "I'll admit that I loved him once. I don't any more."

"Are you sure?"

Kate took out her keys. "Thanks for the dinner, Roger. I'm going in the shop to finish up a few things. I'll give you a call soon."

She turned to look at him to see if he was going to give her a kiss. But his gaze was fixed straight ahead on the reflection of his headlights in the window of Golden Needles.

Kate sat in the half-lit shop and leaned on the counter. She'd watched Roger's car drive away with a sense of self-inflicted loss. Roger's question had been a legitimate one, and instead of answering it clearly and firmly, she'd run away. She knew why she hadn't answered. It was because the Nick she had seen tonight at the restaurant had been the man she had always hoped he'd someday become.

He'd drifted through college earning average grades without trying very hard and spending more time partying than worrying about the future. By the time she'd met him, he'd dropped out after his first year and a half of law school and was working when he felt like it for his father's construction company. They met at a party given by a mutual friend and found they shared a common interest in art, which had been one of the few subjects Nick had actually paid attention to in college.

Looking back, that seemed like a slender thread to hold two such different people together. In the years since he'd left, Kate had come to the conclusion that more important than what they'd had in common were their differences. They'd been the perfect union of opposites. She was dedicated—driven, really—to getting somewhere in life, while Nick was always at a loss as to whether there was anywhere worthwhile to go. Something about her desire to succeed had appealed to him, and something of his casual pleasure in floating through life had struck a responsive chord in her.

When he'd asked her to marry him she'd accepted, dreamily picturing them sailing along happily on her income and his personality. But he'd hurt her deeply with his sudden decision to go west. The enthusiasm that showed in his eyes as he had discussed his plans to find himself had proven that he could cast her aside with careless indifference when her needs conflicted with his own selfish interest.

Over time, as the hurt lessened, Kate had counted herself lucky that Nick hadn't married her. Opposites might strike sparks, but that usually led to a fire that burned fast and hot but didn't last long. She could imagine herself in middle age, an embittered woman constantly nagging her boy-husband who had never grown up—a husband who probably would take his sense of hurt and shame into the arms of another woman for consolation. That wasn't a future; it was a nightmare.

But *this* Nick, the one she had seen tonight. Could someone change so completely, or was it only appearances? Kate shook her head. This wasn't the moment for thinking about it. The morning would be soon enough for that, when time had brought things into clearer focus. But she knew that if she went home she'd toss in bed or sit in the chair remembering the past and brooding on the future. She had to do something.

Kate had stopped by the realtors that afternoon and made an offer on the house. At the same time, Kate had asked the realtor if she could go into the house and take some measurements to see if the shelves and counter from her current store would fit in the new retail area. At first the realtor said that she'd have to accompany Kate, but after a quick call to Dagmar, who was delighted that Kate had made an offer, the realtor offered Kate a key, saying that the electricity was still on and the heat was working just enough to keep the pipes from freezing through the winter.

Why not go over there now? Kate thought, excited at the prospect of seeing her new home for the first time all by herself. *It will take my mind off of Nick and Roger.* She went in the back room of the shop and got her tape measure. She carefully measured the length and width of the counter, the dimensions of her supply shelves, and the size of her fabric aisles. That done, she tucked a flashlight in her pocket just in case and was on her way.

When she arrived at the house, she sat by the curb and just looked. She realized for the first time how impressive it actually was: a dark, substantial presence against the lighter darkness of the sky. She went up the walk listening to the wind rattling through the bare branches high up in the trees. Up on the front porch, Kate was glad that she'd brought her flashlight in order to find the keyhole in the large double front door.

Once the door had opened with a loud squeak—
have to put some oil on that, Kate thought—she fumbled around on the right and finally found the light
switch. One switch did nothing. Probably hooked up
to some outlets where Dagmar had used lamps, Kate
figured. The other switch turned on an overhead light
that filled the hall and front room with yellowish light.
That would have to be modified. Good lighting was
essential to any fabric store so customers could see
true colors without stepping outside all the time.

The front room seemed large even at night. A few
quick measurements assured Kate that she would have
almost double the retail space in her new quarters.
Imagining how she would arrange her material, Kate
drifted into the back room, the former dining room,
which had been used as a workspace. This long room
with six large windows to the east would be a wonderful area. The lighting might have to be improved,
but it would allow her to have large classes.

Kate was in the rear of the house, surveying Dagmar's former kiln room and trying to decide how to
adapt if for fabric painting, when she heard a noise:
the squeaking of the front door. It wasn't as loud as
it had been when she had opened it, but softer, more
stealthy, as if someone was trying to enter without
being heard.

Kate froze. No one should be in the house but her.
Should she try to get out through the kitchen? She
wasn't sure where the door was, but there had to be
one. The question was whether she could open it from
the inside without a key.

Kate decided that getting trapped in the kitchen

seemed less appealing than confronting the intruder at the front door. *It will also look less foolish if it turns out to be only a curious neighbor checking on who's here,* she thought. She looked up and on the shelf above her head saw a crudely shaped pot. Apparently Dagmar had dabbled in something other than dolls. It was small enough that Kate could easily throw it if that became necessary.

"Hello," Kate called out, edging down the hall to the front room, armed with her pot. She hoped that if it was a burglar they'd be scared off by finding a person in the house. She heard the front door squeak again as if someone were leaving.

Kate walked down the hall more rapidly. As she reached the front door a car engine started out by the street. As she ran onto the porch a red sports car raced away, taking the corner with screeching wheels.

Kate leaned against the porch post. Her body was shaking from fear and anger. Frustrated, she squeezed the pot in her hands as if trying to change its shape. If it isn't Melissa doing this, then who is it, she asked herself, angry tears coming to her eyes. And now they know about my new house. Are they going to try to sabotage that next? Roger and the realtor were the only two people in town who knew about her intention to purchase this house. How could Melissa have found out?

Suddenly tired, she pushed the thought away. She went inside and turned out the lights, then locked the door. There would be time for everything in the morning.

Chapter Fifteen

"They're lovely," Sandy said as the smiling delivery man placed the flowers on the counter in front of Kate.

"Yes, aren't they," Kate said. She tried to sound calm, but her breathing was rushed as she opened the card that had come with them.

Dearest Kate,
I hope you believe that people can change. I hope
you believe in new beginnings.

Love,
Nick

"From an admirer?" Sandy asked with a grin.
"Just an old friend."
"I wish I had old friends like that."
Two weeks had passed since she had run into Nick

in the restaurant. Kate had started to think that his talk of staying in touch was nothing more than politeness. Her first sense of surprise and excitement had lessened into a mixture of disappointment and relief as the days had gone by without hearing from him. But all of it came back now in a flash.

"I'm going to take them in the back room. We can't have the place looking like a funeral home," Kate said. *And I don't want to have people asking me who sent the flowers,* she thought.

The phone rang almost as soon as she had settled behind her desk.

"Did you get my flowers?"

No name, no "hello," Kate thought. Just assuming that after two years she would immediately recognize his voice. There was that old streak of arrogance that had alternately irritated and fascinated her. Going out with Nick was a bit like being with royalty. He always expected to be treated as someone special, and surprisingly often that expectation was enough to make it happen. Hostesses gave him the best table at restaurants where Kate most likely would end up having to pay. Special consideration came from charmed sales women in department stores where Kate would buy him gifts. Even men found Nick's brand of self-confidence attractive, so he never lacked for partners willing to pay his way on the golf course or the tennis court.

How a man who had never accomplished much of anything was able to go along treating people as if he were to the manor born had always been a mystery to Kate—until she'd met Nick's family. As the only boy, his mother and three sisters treated him like a prince, and his father continued to fondly hope that Nick would succeed him one day as head of his construction company.

"Yes, I did receive them. The flowers are very nice. Thank you," Kate said, forcing her mind back to the present.

"And what's your response to my note?" Nick asked.

Kate paused. "I think that sometimes people can change. And once in a while it's possible to have new beginnings. It all depends."

"On what?"

Kate could hear the amusement in Nick's voice. He'd always liked verbal flirting. She'd seen him practice it often enough, on herself and on others. Nick flirted the way most men breathed. When they'd been together, she'd convinced herself that it only meant something when he did it with her. At any rate, that was what he told her when she had complained about his attentions to other women. Finally she'd dismissed his continual need to impress every attractive woman he met as an attempt to compensate for not yet having achieved much in life. Would a law degree have changed that? she wondered.

"It depends on whether the change is for real."

"Then how about we get together for dinner, and I begin my campaign to convince you that my metamorphosis is complete?"

"Not tonight, Nick. I'm teaching a class."

"I could stop by and watch."

Kate laughed at the thought of Nick watching a

group of women quilt. He'd flirt so outrageously that they'd end up sewing the quilts to their clothes.

"You'd be too much of a distraction."

"I'm glad you think so. How about tomorrow night, then? I could take you back to Diavolo's or somewhere even better."

"That would be pretty expensive for a recent law school grad, unless you have received a good job offer."

"Don't worry, Kate, the sky's the limit for me now."

"How about lunch tomorrow at the luncheonette right up from my shop?"

Nick was silent for a moment. "That's not very romantic."

"I know. But remember, the last time we met for a meal you broke our engagement. That didn't leave me in a very romantic mood."

"Ah, you have a point," he said without a trace of shame. "Tomorrow for lunch then."

"Fine."

"And, Kate."

"What?"

"I hope that I can get you back in the mood."

Kate hung up the phone torn between anger and anticipation. How often she'd felt that way with Nick. Was that a road she wanted to go down again? Lunch tomorrow would tell. She'd been foolish to believe his promises the first time, and she'd be doubly foolish if she made the same mistake again. Nick would have to prove beyond the shadow of a doubt that he had changed.

Kate went out to the front counter just as the door

opened and Roger came into the shop. They had talked on the phone several times since their disastrous dinner but hadn't gotten together again. The Christmas season was in full swing and Roger was worked off his feet trying to manage the store without an assistant, while Kate's own schedule had gone from difficult to impossible.

They'd both apologized over the phone for how the night at the restaurant had gone. He said that he'd been childishly jealous, and she admitted to letting an old friend take too much of her attention away from the person she was with. But she knew that Roger was still waiting for an answer to his question about whether she still loved Nick before he would invite her out again. Maybe after the lunch tomorrow she'd be able to answer it.

Oh, great! Kate thought when she saw the solemn expression on Roger's face. *At least when there were no men in my life, I could concentrate on the shop. Now it seems that there are emotional traumas around every corner. Would I trade the boring past for the exciting present?* she asked herself. *Nah!* she replied quickly.

Sandy scurried away to a far corner of the shop and began busying herself with the bolts of fabric.

"I have to talk with you," Roger said. His mouth formed a thin tense line.

"Okay."

"Who's she," he whispered, indicating Sandy.

"A part-time employee."

"She looks kind of familiar. Can we go in your back room?"

Kate led the way into the back. It was only when she was behind her desk and Roger was occupying the only other chair in the room that she realized that Nick's flowers dominated the center of her desk.

"Did someone send you flowers?" Roger asked with a twisted smile.

"Yes. Nick."

Roger grunted. "Let's forget about him for the moment if we can. We've got problems with Melissa again. She's managed to convince her father that she would do better at learning the business if he transferred us both to a new store that's opening in Colorado. It's much larger, and she's saying that it would give her more to do. Right now, she claims, I'm running things and leaving her with only menial tasks. She didn't tell her father that she isn't bothering to do even the menial tasks I've assigned her. He's so excited that she's interested in the business that he'll give her anything she wants."

"She couldn't drive me out of business, so now she's decided that the only way to get us apart is to have you relocated," Kate said.

She could feel her anger toward Melissa rising. How dare she meddle in people's lives so willfully?

"What are you going to do?" she asked Roger.

He reached over and took her hand.

"It would help me to decide if I knew how you felt. I realize that we haven't actually known each other long, but sometimes . . . well, sometimes it feels to me as if it's been years."

Kate gave his hand a squeeze. "I like you a lot

Roger, but I need more time before I can be certain of whether we have a future together."

"Is it because of him?" Roger asked, waving his hand in the direction of the flowers as if he'd like to sweep them off the desk.

"No, not really," Kate said slowly. "Even if Nick had never come back, I would feel that we need more time to get to know each other before making a commitment. How much time do we have?"

"Not enough. Melissa's father is coming out here for Christmas, and he's bringing the new manager with him. Melissa and I are supposed to transfer by the first of the year."

"So soon," Kate groaned, then she brightened. "You could quit your job with Fabulous Fabrics. You'd be able to find something around here that would give you enough to live on. You could even help me get my fabric painting business up and running."

Roger gave a wan smile. "That's a nice thought. The money doesn't matter to me. I'd do it in a minute if it weren't for my family."

"I don't know how to say this, and it will probably come out wrong," she said hesitantly. "But there is such a thing as being too unselfish."

"What do you mean?" he asked sharply.

"It's true that your family did send you through college, but that was when your father was alive and working. I'm sure your brother and sisters don't expect you to give up everything to support them."

"But they deserve it," he replied quickly. "It's not their fault that Dad died when he did. I don't deserve to be the only lucky one."

Kate put her hand on his arm. "You should help them, I'm not denying that. But you're trying awfully hard to be a father to them when you're only the older brother. Maybe you should ask them how they feel about that."

Roger pulled his arm away. "Family is important, Kate. I don't want them graduating with huge college debts that it will take them years to pay back."

"And maybe they don't want to owe a huge debt of gratitude to you that they won't ever be able to pay back."

"I'll think about what you've said," Roger said after a long pause. "I know that I've got an important decision to make here." He looked at the flowers. "But I think you've got some deciding to do too."

Kate could barely keep her eyes open by the time the quilting class finally ended at nine o'clock that night. With only a week left until Christmas, it seemed as though everything still remained to be done. She hadn't started her Christmas shopping for her mother and Rhonda, or for Harry and Roger, the recent additions to her list. There were two more classes scheduled for the week, plus she had to finish her quilt for the show that was going to be displayed the day before Christmas.

As she wearily locked the door of the shop and climbed into her van, the one piece of good news she could think of was that the vandalism against her shop had stopped. No new incidents in the last two weeks, not since the intruder at her house-to-be. *That just lends more support to my view that Melissa is behind it,* Kate said to herself. *Melissa goes to Colorado and the problems stop. Of course, the incident at the gray house, when the intruder had pulled away in a red sports car, had occurred after Melissa returned to Denver. But somehow Melissa was behind it. I don't know how, but she was,* Kate thought stubbornly. *The events fit together too neatly for it to be a coincidence.*

Kate pulled out of the parking lot, about to head for home, when she remembered that there was no milk in the house. Deciding she had to have some for her breakfast in the morning, Kate turned the other way to go to the convenience store. She rushed through the store grabbing a half-gallon of milk and adding a loaf of bread for good measure. It seemed to her that the slice she'd toasted this morning had been a bit green around the edges.

She was sitting in the van, waiting to pull out into traffic, when she saw someone who looked very much like Nick coming out the door of the elegant German restaurant across the street. He was holding hands with a blond woman, who leaned towards him and laughed as the man gestured and talked in an animated fashion. Kate blinked, checking to be sure. She was certain. It was Nick. The light in front of the building was bright, and his every movement had long ago been wired into her brain. As if to make sure there was no opportunity for Kate to delude herself, the couple stopped right under the streetlight and kissed.

Kate stepped on the gas and flew out into the traffic, barely missing an oncoming truck. She pushed the accelerator to the floor, causing the van's engine to shudder in protest. When she'd gone half a mile, she slowed down.

What am I running away from? she asked herself. *He's the one who should be ashamed. He fooled me once, and almost as soon as he comes back to town, he's doing it again.*

By the time Kate had pulled into the driveway at home, she knew why she felt ashamed of herself. It was because she clearly hadn't grown up as much as she'd thought she had. All Nick had to do was say a few nice things and flash his smile, and she'd come running, even though the last time he had kicked her in the teeth. *Do I have so little respect for myself that I enjoy being mistreated?* she asked herself, slamming the van door.

Kate stomped up the stairs, starting up the pain in her sore ankle again. When she got into her apartment, she dropped the milk and bread on the sofa and picked up the phone. Then she put it down again and circled the room for several minutes.

She'd been ready to call Nick and leave a scathing message on his answering machine, but the thought of exposing her anger to Nick seemed the wrong thing to do. "You shouldn't show emotion to people who don't care about you," her mother had often said. And for the first time, Kate understood what that really meant. Her outrage was her last shred of dignity, and she planned to hold onto it.

As he had always done, Nick was living with his family, but he had his own private line. Apparently his parents had kept it for him even during his years in California because that was the number Nick had written on the card with his flowers. Kate called and as expected got his machine. She left a short message politely expressing her regrets, and saying that something had come up and she wouldn't be able to make their lunch tomorrow.

After she hung up the phone, Kate knew that she had done the right thing. Confronting Nick would only lead to more of his lies and excuses. He'd say the girl was a blind date that his sister had set up for him, so what could he do? He'd even make kissing the woman somehow sound altruistic. By the time he would explain the events to Kate in all of their improbable detail, he might even start to believe the trumped-up story himself.

The only way to handle Nick was to banish him from her world. As far as Kate was concerned, he had never come home.

Chapter Sixteen

Kate spent much of the next morning working with several women who had taken classes over the last month but had not finished their projects. Since it was the day before Christmas, they were now desperate for assistance to complete quilts that they were planning to give as Christmas gifts. Quilt tops ready to be tied to their Polyfil and backing piece were spread out over the floor of the shop. Anxious workers were desperately pushing needles with embroidery thread through them and tying knots on the top of the quilt.

Fortunately, Sandy was done with school for the semester and had been willing to put in the entire day. She handled the phone and dealt with the other customers while Kate tried to calm the busy quilters. Finally, by one o'clock, most of the projects had been finished. Kate let Sandy go to lunch, and she sat down wearily behind the counter with a container of yogurt in hand. The phone rang.

"Hi!" someone said cheerfully when Kate answered.

Kate couldn't quite place the familiar voice.

"It's Rhonda. Have you forgotten me already?"

"Of course not, but you sound different."

"That's probably because I'm happy."

"Good for you," Kate said. "Someone planning to get married in less than two months should be happy."

"It's been great. I met Travis's parents. They're thrilled about Travis and me. They think it's wonderful that he's finally got a girlfriend who's mature and well balanced."

"Ah," Kate said, wondering what Travis's previous girlfriends must have been like.

"And it turns out that his folks have got scads of money."

"I thought Travis was a struggling surfboard maker."

"Yeah. Well, his folks sort of cut him off because of some of the things he's done. Nothing really bad, but you know how parents can be. Anyway, now that they've met me everything is back to normal. His dad is going to give him enough money to get his business off the ground."

"That's really wonderful," Kate said.

"So I don't want you worrying about sending me the money for Golden Needles. I may never need it."

Kate explained about getting the money from her mother and told Rhonda about moving Golden Needles to a new location.

"So I'll be able to send you the money from your

share of the business before you get married," Kate concluded.

Rhonda was silent for a moment.

"Is anything wrong?" Kate asked.

"Nope. I guess that hearing about your plans just made me realize that my life there with you is really over. As long as I owned part of Golden Needles, I could always come back. Now I guess I'm committed to my life out here."

"Are you sure you're all right with that?"

"Oh, yeah. But change is scary, you know? It's always easier to go along in the same old rut, especially when it's a comfortable one."

"Well, no matter what happens," Kate said, "you'll have a place to stay with me. And I can use some help around the shop anytime."

"Thanks, Kate. You've always been a good friend."

"Nick is back in town," Kate blurted out. She wasn't sure why she'd said it. She hadn't intended to tell Rhonda. Maybe it was all this talk about friendship; she really needed to discuss Nick with someone who knew him and was a friend.

"That toad!" Rhonda almost screamed.

"You always said he was cute," Kate reminded her. In fact there had been a time when Kate had thought Rhonda was a bit jealous of her relationship with Nick.

"A guy can be cute and still be a toad," Rhonda said. "He practically dumped you at the altar, Kate. You aren't thinking about seeing him again, are you?"

"He's got his law degree. He says that he's changed."

"Toads don't change." Rhonda paused. "Well, they

may go from being tadpoles to toads, but once they're really toads, they stay toads. And that's what Nick is. You stay away from him, Kate. He pushes your buttons and you do stupid things. I wish I were there to keep you out of trouble."

Kate almost laughed but didn't want to hurt her friend's feelings.

"You know what, Rhonda," Kate said, when she got her voice under control.

"What?"

"You've always been a good friend too."

No sooner had Kate put down the phone than it rang again.

"I'm sorry we couldn't get together for lunch today," Nick said as soon as she answered. "I was looking forward to it."

I saw how much you were looking forward to it last night, Kate wanted to say but remembered her promise to herself.

"This is such a busy time of year," she replied vaguely.

"Are you going to the Christmas Eve Chamber of Commerce Ball tonight?"

"I suppose." As a small business owner and a member of the Chamber, she bought a ticket every year. But she'd been so busy and upset recently that the ball, held at the local country club, had completely slipped her mind. She wondered if Roger would be going.

"Save the first dance for me," Nick was saying in her ear.

"I'll try."

"And, Kate," he said in the deep voice he always

slipped into when he had a romantic proposal to make. "I was wondering if you'd like to go with me up to Vermont for a little ski trip over the holidays. A friend is loaning me his lodge for a few days."

"Gee, Nick. I'll have to see," Kate said, barely able to control her anger. Was the blond busy? she wondered. "I was planning to close the store for only two days after Christmas to visit my mom."

"Why not close for the whole week? How much business does your little shop usually do in a day, anyhow?" Kate heard a familiar petulance in his voice.

"I'll let you know," she said, forcing herself to sound calm.

"Fine. See you tonight."

Kate unfolded the quilt she was going to enter in the Christmas Eve Quilt Show. She still had to sew the sleeve on the back to hang it by. Double wedding ring: what a beautiful traditional pattern, Kate thought. Just like marriage, it represents two separate people who have chosen to intertwine their lives forever. Sure, it was a little corny, but was what guys like Nick were offering really better? Fun without responsibility; laughs without love.

Kate picked up the phone and dialed the Fabulous Fabrics number. She finally got Roger on the line.

"Kate," he said in a pleased voice. "It's great to hear from you. Sorry I haven't called in a couple of days, but I've been up to my ears around here."

"Me, too. Look I just wanted to check on whether you were planning to go to the Chamber of Commerce Ball tonight."

"I plan to. Melissa and her father arrived this morning. I want to find some time to speak with Stan alone later on in the afternoon, but after that I should be free. The store is closing at five."

"What are you going to tell Melissa's father?" Kate asked.

Roger paused. "You know, I took your advice and laid things out for my family. I gave them kind of a quick rundown on what's been going on with Melissa. They thought I should have quit a long time ago."

"The money thing didn't bother them?"

"My sisters are planning to go to the state university, so Mom can afford that with a little help from me. And my brother said that he was waiting for a chance to help pay some of his own way. He said that I'd been trying to be his father for too long and I should start being his brother again."

"That's great. Sounds like you've got a wonderful family."

"Yeah. They are pretty good, at that. Since Dad's death I guess I'd forgotten that we've always made a pretty good team. Anyway, I'm going to tell Stan what's been happening and let him know that if he wants a chaperone for Melissa, he'll have to find someone else."

"Well, whatever happens, Roger, come to the ball. I'll be saving the first dance for you."

"Does that mean you're ready to answer my question?"

"Absolutely."

"Wonderful," Roger said, and she could tell by the warmth in his voice that he had guessed her answer.

Kate was smiling to herself as she sewed the sleeve

on the back of the quilt. The shop bell rang as Sandy came back from lunch. She looked around the shop to make sure no one was there.

"This is my last day, Kate."

"I know. You said that you'd be going home for the holidays. When will you be back for the spring semester?"

"That's the thing, I won't."

"Why not?"

Sandy shrugged. "Things just didn't work out for me here. I figure that I'll go back to Boston. Maybe I'll go to school there."

From the expression on the girl's face, Kate could tell that she didn't want to be asked any questions.

"Well, if you do come back here to school, I'd be happy to have you working for me."

Sandy nodded and looked down at the floor.

"I guess you won't be at the quilt show tomorrow. You'll probably be spending Christmas Day with your parents," Kate said.

Sandy shook her head. "My folks are going to visit my brother down in Maryland. I'm going to get to-gether with some friends from school who live around here. I'll try to catch the show."

Kate checked her watch.

"Well, it's almost two-thirty. I promised the women in the quilt guild that I'd lend a hand in helping them set up the show. How about we close up the shop? If you want to help me set up the show, you can come along. It's just up the block at the banquet room at the Inn. I'll pay you for your time."

Sandy nodded. Just then the door opened and Tim

walked into the shop. He'd been coming by at least once a week to look around the shop and chat with Kate. She knew he'd had his eye on a quilted wall hanging of a Christmas tree that had real lights that blinked on and off. They were operated by a small battery pack concealed in a pocket sewn into the back of the quilt.

"I'm glad you stopped by," Kate said as the boy walked into the store. "How would you like to help me set up a quilt show?"

"I guess. What do I have to do?"

Kate explained. "And in return for helping me, I'll give you that Christmas tree quilt."

"Really!"

"Sure. You'll have earned it."

Kate locked up the store and the three of them piled into her van for the short drive to the Inn. The Cranford Inn was an old rambling building. One side of the structure was given over to a restaurant that boasted real New England food. The center part of the building was a small lobby and reception desk with stairs leading up to a dozen or so rooms. To the left was a large rectangular banquet room. Frequently used by local people for marriage receptions, graduation parties, and charitable banquets, the room was what enabled the Inn to survive.

Kate could see that members of her quilt guild had already begun assembling the wooden racks from which the bed-sized quilts would hang. Piles of quilts covered a row of tables under the front windows.

"You're here just in time," Aurora Watts, the president of the guild, said when she saw Kate. "And you've brought some help. Young, healthy help!"

Kate glanced around and noted that all the ladies at work attempting to hang the quilts were well into their sixties and beyond.

"Young man, can you give me a hand here?" one woman old enough to be his great grandmother called to Tim. With a parting grin at Kate, he went over to help.

Pretty soon Sandy and Kate were also working with small teams putting the heavy quilts on the racks and organizing the display into rows. Two hours later the show was completely hung and the twenty or so volunteers were resting by the door into the banquet room drinking hot cider provided by the Inn. One older woman was trying without much success to get Tim to try some of her homemade fruitcake.

"This is our biggest show ever," Aurora said to Kate. "It will make the job of the judges even harder."

Unlike most small quilt shows which are not judged, Kate's guild always had outside judges with good credentials to award ribbons. Kate had placed second last year. She was hoping that this year her double wedding ring quilt would have a chance at a first-place blue ribbon, but she'd noticed several other quilts that seemed equally good. At least hers was in a good location, at the end of the aisle facing the door.

"When are the judges coming through?" she asked Aurora.

"They should be here by six. Probably they'll be done by eight. But, of course, no one will know who won what until tomorrow at one, when we open."

Kate nodded. The show only opened officially on the afternoon of Christmas Day. It stayed open until the evening of the day after Christmas. Some younger members of the guild had objected recently that since people often traveled on Christmas, it would be better if the show were held a few weeks before or after the holiday. But tradition had prevailed, and as Aurora often said, the show gave people who didn't have families to visit something to do. Kate figured she'd run up to Vermont right after seeing the show.

"Well, isn't this just so typically New England," an icy voice behind Kate said loudly. "A little quilt show on the holiday."

Kate knew by the voice that Melissa was back. The woman brushed past her and walked into the banquet room. Wearing a red silk blouse, tight black jeans, and boots with stiletto heels, she turned, once she was well into the room, to look back at the crowd of women gawking at her from the doorway.

One of Santa's evil helpers, Kate thought. She could feel sorry for Melissa in the abstract, but whenever the woman stood before her in the flesh, anger always dominated.

"Why, Kate, how nice to see you again," Melissa said, feigning surprise. "I'll bet you have some little creation of yours here. Do show it to me."

Kate pointed at the quilt next to where Melissa was standing.

Melissa stared, and for a moment Kate would have sworn that even she was impressed.

"How nice," she finally said, "but oh so traditional. And those wedding rings, I'm afraid you aren't going to be getting one of those any time soon. At least not from you-know-who."

Melissa's eyes fixed on Kate as she smiled cruelly.

"It's so sad when we hope for something and just when it's within our grasp, it's snatched away. The disappointment can be so overwhelming."

Melissa doesn't know that Roger isn't going to move, Kate realized. *I could tell her now, but why create a scene in front of my friends?*

"Yes, Melissa. Disappointment can be a terrible thing," Kate said, smiling serenely as if Melissa's comments had nothing to do with her.

Melissa stared at her. Her smug smiled faltered for a moment.

"Will you be at the dance tonight?" she asked Kate.

"Of course."

"I'll see you there. It will be a good time for saying good-byes."

Melissa marched back through the crowd of still gaping women, who quickly made way for her. She went into the lobby and up the stairs to the rooms above. *So she and her father are staying here,* Kate thought. *I guess they want to absorb some of the local color.*

"Who was that?" Aurora asked in amazement.

"Just another woman in the fabric business," Kate replied.

"My word, she certainly is . . ." Aurora seemed at a loss for the proper adjective.

"Dramatic," Kate suggested.

"That too," Aurora replied, showing more wit than Kate would ever have expected.

Chapter Seventeen

After returning to the shop to give Tim his quilt, Kate rushed to a nearby mall and braved the mobs of last-minute shoppers. She bought a scarf for Rhonda, promising herself that she'd mail it out next week. It wouldn't get there until a few days after Christmas, but since Rhonda herself never purchased Christmas gifts until after the first of the year—a way of avoiding the commercialization of the holiday, she claimed—it wouldn't matter.

Kate found an appropriately masculine sweater for Harry. For her mother, Kate's gift was going to be the offer to make a quilt for the bed in her new home. They could go over to Harry's farm over the holidays and decide on fabrics and colors. It would be fun for them to do it together.

But what to get Roger? Kate sat on one of the few empty seats and watched the crowd swirl past. Everything she could think of was either too simple to capture all the feelings she wanted to express, or far too elaborate for her limited budget. Suddenly she spied a bakery across the way. She dodged through the crowd and looked in the window. Wonderful cakes of all sizes were on display. Now there was an idea! she thought.

By the time Kate got home it was almost eight. The ball always began with a large buffet starting at eight. The band usually arrived soon after and dancing began by nine. Kate shoved through her closet looking for her one good evening dress. She'd worn the same one last year, but that wouldn't matter because Roger hadn't seen it. Kate thought the shade of green went well with her dark brown hair and light complexion, and it reflected a little of the holiday season.

It was almost eight-thirty by the time she handed her keys to the valet, who glanced at her battered van with dismay before driving it away. *Probably plans to hide it behind the BMWs and Volvos,* Kate thought.

She strode quickly up the steps to the country club and through the front entrance. She checked her coat and went into the room where the rattle of silverware told her the buffet was in progress. Kate paused in the doorway, looking to see who was there. If pressed she probably could have identified almost everyone in the room, but there were several she was particularly interested in spotting.

Across the room, she immediately noticed Melissa, resplendent in a backless red sheath. She was standing next to a short, blocky older man who might well have been her father. He was looking around him sternly as if unhappy about something. Kate smiled to herself, Melissa certainly could have that effect on people. Closer to her she saw Nick's mother and sisters. Standing with them was someone who looked very much like the young woman she'd seen with Nick last night. Could Nick be far behind? Even Jack Martinson was there, with a glass of champagne in one hand and what looked to be an antacid mint in the other.

"Are you in charge of security?" Roger asked, suddenly appearing next to her. "You seem to be scanning the room."

"I was just thinking how many of the people who have been thorns in my side are in this room right now," she replied.

"I hope I'm not included in that number."

"Not at all." She seized his arm and pulled him into a corner away from the crowd.

"So you've talked to Melissa's father by now. What happened?"

"You are looking at the newest member of the ranks of the unemployed."

Kate stood on her toes and quickly kissed Roger on the lips.

"What's this? Do you have a thing for guys without a job? I wish I'd known that sooner, I'd have quit weeks ago."

"I'm just proud of the fact that you stood up to him."

Roger frowned. "Stan did get pretty angry. He didn't want to think that even Melissa would stoop so low as to try to blackmail someone into going out with her. He was even less happy at the thought that she wasn't serious about being in the business. I guess he'd been staking a lot on that. He kept refusing to hear what I was telling him."

"You mean he didn't believe you?"

"He had the look of a man who half believes but doesn't really want to accept it. When I told him that I wasn't going to move, I think he was actually sorry at having to let me go."

"He should be. You're one of his best employees."

Roger put his arm around Kate's waist and gave her a squeeze. "My biggest supporter," he said. Then he looked down into her eyes. "And what about the question I asked you several weeks ago?"

Kate smiled up at him. "I am absolutely sure that I do not love Nick."

This time the hug he gave her took her breath away.

"I'm very happy to hear that," he whispered in her ear.

"But I do have to speak with Nick," Kate said.

"He's here tonight," Roger said. "In fact he had the nerve to come up to me and ask if I'd seen you. Apparently he wants to talk with you about something."

"Don't get jealous if you see him talking to me. I can assure you that this will be the last time I have anything to say to him."

"I can't promise not to get jealous, but I'll leave Nick to you. I can tell at a glance that you're up to handling him."

They wandered over to the buffet and filled their plates. Several people came up to Kate, and she introduced them to Roger, telling them with great pleasure that he was planning to settle permanently in town.

That frequently led to discussions as to whether he was married and what neighborhood would be good to search for a place to live.

"Be careful," Kate warned when they were alone. "Most everyone here has an unmarried daughter or sister, and they all have friends in the real estate business."

Roger smiled. "Forewarned is forearmed. I see a couple of guys I know from the Chamber of Commerce. I think I'll go over and do a little networking now that I'm looking for a job. See you once the dancing starts."

Kate watched Roger move through the crowd. A number of women cast surreptitious glances his way as he went past. Kate decided that she wasn't going to leave Roger alone any longer than she had to in this shark tank.

"Hello, Kate," said Nick's mother, sailing through the crowd. "How wonderful to see you again. You've been a stranger for far too long."

The mother and four sisters all gathered in front of Kate, chattering and smiling sincerely as if they were completely unaware of what Nick had done to her two years ago.

Perhaps they were, Kate suddenly realized. Who knew how Nick had distorted the truth to his family? Two years ago, he might well have told them that he and Kate had ended their engagement by mutual agreement, with both of them relieved and happy to have avoided marriage. The truth was like modeling clay to Nick; he could mold it into any shape he wanted.

Nick's mother motioned for the blond woman Kate had seen with Nick last night to come over from a nearby group to be introduced. Kate could see that she was even more attractive than she had thought, with porcelain skin and high cheekbones. Only her nose, which seemed a bit long, kept her from being truly beautiful, but Kate figured that her own perspective might not be quite objective. The elegant black dress she was wearing, on the other hand, Kate had no reservations about. It was stunning.

"This is Catherine Bafford," Nick's mother said. "Her father is Judge Leo Bafford. Leo is an old friend of my husband's. He's helping Nick search for a position in Boston."

Kate knew from Nick that because his father was in construction he had many connections in Boston. Now it looked like they were paying off. Kate wondered if going out with the judge's daughter was what Nick had to do to get a job or whether that was a cozy side benefit.

The woman gave Kate a graceful nod. Kate hoped that her little return bow was equally poised. Catherine certainly exuded elegance. How elegant will she be the first time she catches Nick in a parking lot with another woman? Kate wondered.

The music had started up in the ballroom, so after a few polite remarks to Nick's family, Kate went across the hall to watch the band. Several older couples were already on the dance floor and the band was well into a lively fox-trot.

Kate felt lips brush the side of her face.

"Hello, Kate," Nick whispered in her ear. "I was

afraid you might not come. And I see you've saved the first dance for me just like you promised."

Kate took a step away from him.

"I wouldn't want to miss the ball. There's so many interesting people here," she said.

"Do you really think so? I've always found the town rather boring."

"Is that why you're planning to go to Boston?"

Nick gave her a sheepish grin. "Ah, you've been talking to my mother. She doesn't believe in keeping secrets. But I am hoping to land a job there. The legal opportunities are so much better. I don't plan to spend my life as a small-town lawyer working on wills and residential real estate."

"I guess you won't have to, especially with the help of a judge."

"My mother has been busy," Nick said. His brow furrowed slightly as it always did when he was annoyed. "But that's how it is in the world. It's not what you know, but who you know."

Kate watched the growing numbers of people moving around the dance floor.

"The judge's daughter is very attractive."

She quickly looked at Nick and saw him trying to calculate how much she knew.

"My mother set that up," he said. "You know how it is with mothers. They're always trying to be matchmakers."

Kate smiled politely.

Nick reached over and took her hand. "But I pick the woman I want to be with. How about that ski trip, Kate, what do you say? I'd really like us to pick up where we left off. I've come to understand a lot over the last two years. One of the things I know now is that not marrying you was the biggest mistake I've ever made."

"Are you proposing to me, Nick?" she asked.

Nick shrugged with embarrassment as if Kate's directness was somehow ill-mannered.

"Let's not rush, Kate, we've got all the time in the world. Why don't we get to know each other again?"

Kate waved her free hand with elegant indifference to show that she wasn't impressed.

"You're right, of course, that would be a step backward," Nick said quickly, judging her mood. "Why don't we get re-engaged but keep it just between us for a while? At least until my job prospects are firmed up."

Kate began to laugh. She couldn't help herself. Suddenly Nick was so transparent that his simplicity was comical.

"What's so funny?" he asked, dropping her hand, clearly hurt and angry. "I really do love you."

She reached over and stroked his cheek gently.

"In your own way I think you do. You're a lovely boy, Nick. With an awful lot of luck, you may someday grow up into a lovely man, and I hope for the sake of whatever woman ends up with you that it happens soon. But one of the things I know now is that not marrying you was the best thing that ever happened to me."

Nick's face twitched for a moment, then he turned and rapidly walked away, blindly bumping into Roger who was standing nearby.

"He didn't appear happy," Roger said.

"He'll get over it."

"What did you two talk about?" he asked cautiously.

"He proposed to me. At least I think he did."

Roger put his hands on both her shoulders and turned Kate so that she directly faced him.

"You can't marry him," he said firmly. "I want to marry you."

"Is that a proposal?" Kate said, smiling innocently. "Two in one night would be quite a treat."

Roger's eyes filled with amusement. "Do you want me to get down on one knee?"

"That's not necessary. I told you before that we don't know each other well enough, but if we both still feel the same way in a few months, then I'll happily accept your proposal even if you're standing on both feet."

"You'll have to turn down Nick, then."

"I already have."

Roger leaned forward to kiss her. Kate put her hands behind Roger's head and pulled him toward her, pressing her lips hard against his.

"I don't think it's going to take very long to find out how we feel," Roger said moments later when they broke to catch their breath.

"Mmmm. It could be you're right," Kate replied. "You can come with me to Rhonda's wedding in February, so you can see how it's done. They're writing their own vows."

Roger rolled his eyes. "Is that the kind of wedding you want? Are we going to have a lot of talk about swearing before father sky and mother earth to always respect each other's needs?"

"I'll be satisfied with the usual words."

"Good." He tore his eyes away from her to take in the dance floor. "Would you like to dance?"

Kate nodded.

Roger led her out onto the floor. She settled into his arms. As they traveled around the floor, the stress of the last few days slowly drained from her body. Kate leaned her head against Roger's chest and closed her eyes. Their bodies seemed to become one as they floated along. With her eyes closed, Kate could almost believe that they were all alone. She was drifting off to where dreams and reality were indistinguishable when a sharp elbow dug into her side. Her eyes opened in angry surprise, and she saw Melissa pass by, dancing with her father. The look of hatred on Melissa's face made Kate shiver.

"Are you cold?" Roger asked, not having seen Melissa.

She shook her head.

"Tired?"

"A little."

"Do you want to go?"

"Would you mind?"

"Not at all."

As they waited in front of the country club for the valet to bring their vehicles around, Kate said, "I have a Christmas present for you. It's in my van."

"I have one for you too," Roger said, reaching in his pocket. "I was just waiting for the appropriate moment when we'd be alone."

He handed her a jewelry box.

"Should I open it now?"

Roger looked up speculatively at the stars. "I think I just saw Santa's sleigh go by, so I'm sure that it's okay."

She slipped off the bow. Inside the box was a necklace with a golden sewing machine as the pendant. In the glow of the street light Kate could see the sparkle of diamonds from several points on the machine.

"It's lovely! And so unique."

"Well, almost everything you put on has something to do with quilting, so I thought you might actually wear this."

"Thank you."

Kate gave him a long kiss that only stopped when she heard her van sputter up next to them.

"I have a gift for you as well," she said, opening the passenger door. She took out the cake box and presented it with a bow to Roger. Giving her a puzzled look, he opened the box.

Across the top of the cake it read: "To My Friendly Enemy: Merry Christmas."

"Not enemies any more," Roger said, folding her in his arms.

"And I think I can find a couple of forks back at my apartment if you'd like to find whether this cake tastes as good as it looks," Kate said.

Roger's eyes sparkled.

"I'm sure it will," he said. "I'm sure it will."

Chapter Eighteen

Kate couldn't believe that the clock read ten-thirty. She'd slept later than she had for years. After Roger had consumed two pieces of cake to her one and declared it to be the best cake he'd ever tasted, they sat on the sofa and softly talked about all that had happened since they'd met. Their discussion was frequently disrupted by long, sleepy kisses.

"I think I'd better go," Roger finally said.

"Huh?" Kate responded, then realized that she had fallen asleep with her head on his chest.

"We've both been working flat out for weeks, and we're just coming down from some emotionally rough decisions. So, although I hate to say it . . ." He gave Kate a final kiss. "I think we both need some sleep."

He had certainly been right about that, Kate thought as she climbed out of bed. An hour later, having had breakfast, Kate felt almost ready to start the day. She called her mother to make last-minute arrangements for her stay.

"So, Katie, how have things worked out with yourself and Roger?" her mother asked.

Kate told her about Roger's decision not to stay at Fabulous Fabrics.

"The man has got character. I told you that, Katie. Not many men would give up both money and the attentions of a beautiful woman to take a chance on winning the woman he loves."

"I know. And he's doing a pretty good job at it. In fact, I was wondering if Roger could come up with me for the next couple of days so he could get to know you and Harry better."

Her mother paused. "Of course he's welcome. But you'd better tell him to bring a suit."

"A suit?"

"The company that's buying the farm would like to take over a few weeks early. They called yesterday. They're willing to pay me fifty thousand more if I'll let them start building here by the second week of January."

Kate could tell from her mother's voice that she could hardly believe what she was saying about the money.

"That means that Harry and I are going to have to move in together by the beginning of next week. His daughters are staying at his farm now, so we thought that maybe this would be the perfect time for us to get married. Since Harry has no sons, we were wondering who would be his best man. We were thinking of asking someone from the church, but if you and Roger are getting serious, maybe he'd be willing to do it. It's only going to be a small wedding, just family and a few close friends."

"I'll ask him. I think he'll be delighted."

"I'll look forward to seeing the two of you this evening. And good luck at the quilt show."

"Thanks. And Mom?"

"What dear?"

"Congratulations to you and Harry."

At one o'clock Kate arrived in the lobby of the Cranford Inn. Roger was going to meet her at the quilt show and had been warned to bring a suit. Kate had gotten permission to leave her van in the Inn parking lot for a couple of days, so she and Roger would leave from there.

The women who were working at the show as hostesses stood in the doorway talking urgently as Kate entered the lobby. When they saw her, they suddenly became quiet. Kate smiled but got only sorrowful stares in return. Finally, Aurora broke through the group and came toward Kate with her hands outstretched.

"I'm so sorry, Kate. We don't know how it happened. There's a call in to the chief of police. This is criminal."

"What is?" Kate asked, feeling her throat begin to tighten. What could have happened now?

Aurora took her arm and slowly led her into the banquet room. She held onto Kate firmly as if afraid that she might collapse. The first thing her eyes saw was the first prize blue ribbon hanging from the bottom of her quilt. Could Aurora really be so concerned that she would faint for joy? But it wasn't her quilt, not quite her quilt. Someone had nearly cut it in half.

"It's barbaric behavior," Aurora said. "We'll find the person who did this and see that person punished to the fullest extent of the law."

Kate found herself leaning on Aurora's arm as she struggled to keep the tears from her eyes.

"Come and sit down, my dear. I'm sure this has been a terrible shock."

Kate allowed herself to be led over to a wooden chair right inside the door.

"Aurora," one of the women in the doorway called. "Should we let people into the show? There's a crowd starting to gather out here and technically it's past opening time."

Aurora looked at Kate.

"The show must go on," Aurora said with an apologetic smile. "Would you like me to take down your quilt?"

"No," Kate said, a sudden angry note of defiance in her voice. "Please keep it up. People should see what someone has done."

Let's find out if the person who I know is responsible for this has the nerve to show up and face me, Kate said to herself.

The crowd began to wander into the show. They stood as if in mourning in front of Kate's quilt as the hostesses told what had happened. They nodded sadly to Kate, who sat there feeling as if she were the next of kin at a wake.

Roger came in the door, his face filled with anger and concern.

"One of the women outside told me what happend. I'm sorry."

"It had to be Melissa who did this," Kate whispered.

"Is there any evidence?"

Kate shook her head. "I don't need evidence. I know."

Two men in uniform came into the room. Kate recognized the older as the chief of police. They went over to examine the quilt. Sandy came in right behind them. She gave Kate a shy wave and went to stand on the other side of the room.

Finally, Kate saw Melissa and her father enter the room. Melissa, wearing a leather outfit, gave Kate a small smile of triumph as she and her father went over to stand in front of the damaged quilt. Kate started out of the chair, determined to confront her, but Roger laid a restraining hand on her shoulder.

"This is horrible," Kate heard the man with Melissa say in a deep voice. "Anyone who would do this has no respect for fabric. No respect for art."

"It's terrible," Melissa echoed without conviction.

"Are you the lady whose quilt was vandalized?" the chief asked, walking over to where Kate was sitting.

"That's right, I'm Kate Manning," she answered, standing up. She felt far too much like a victim sitting down in front of the tall man.

"What do you know so far?" Roger asked quickly.

The Chief looked at Roger. "Who are you?"

"I'm her friend."

The chief turned his attention back to Kate. "What

we know right now is mostly what the girl at the desk in the lobby told us. The judges left at about eight-fifteen last night. She locked the door at nine. After that there's no one at the desk. Someone is on switchboard all night, but they sit in the back room."

"So you think the vandal got in here between eight-fifteen and nine when the door was locked?" Roger asked.

"Seems like it."

"It couldn't have been Melissa then," Roger said to Kate. "I saw her arrive at the ball right at eight, and she was circulating around the room all through the buffet hour."

"Who's this Melissa?" the chief asked.

"Her," Kate said nodding in the woman's direction.

"Doesn't look like the type," the chief said, looking at Melissa and taking in her expensive outfit at a glance.

"You don't know her," Kate said.

"Would she have a reason?" the chief asked.

Kate nodded. "But I don't have any proof."

"Well, don't go making any accusations about her without proof. Depending on the value of that quilt, this could be a felony. If you start making wild charges, that's . . ." the Chief said.

"Slander. I know," Kate said.

She saw Melissa on the other side of the room pretending to look at the quilts but actually enjoying the whole scene. *This is part of the pleasure for her,* Kate thought, *being able to parade around in front of me knowing that I know she did this, but I can't accuse her without sounding crazy and getting into trouble.*

"Kate." She heard someone call frantically from the doorway.

Tim stood there hopping from foot to foot.

"Can you loan me five dollars so I can get in?" he asked.

Kate nodded.

"I'll take care of it," Roger said.

Tim rushed up to Kate as soon as his hand had been stamped by the elderly woman sitting at the desk outside the door.

"I saw that red car again last night," he burst out. "I didn't know how to get in touch with you, so I came over here."

"Where did you see it?" Kate asked.

"It was in front of your store. By the time I reached the street, the person pulled out and drove up the street. I thought I'd lost it for sure, but then the car pulled right into the parking lot here."

"Did you see who was driving?" Kate asked.

"Sure. She got out of the car and walked right up to the front door. I followed, keeping kind of far back like. She slipped into the lobby when the woman at the desk went into the back for something. I stayed outside. About five minutes later she came out again."

"Who was it?" Kate asked. She couldn't wait to see the expression on Melissa's face when confronted by a witness.

"It was her. The one who works in your store," Tim said, turning to point at her. "It was Sandy."

The other uniformed officer went over to the corner where Sandy was standing like a deer caught in the headlights of a car. As she was brought over to stand by the chief, most of the people in the room seemed to sense that something important was happening, and they began to form a large circle around the chief.

"Did you do this to my quilt?" Kate asked before the chief could put a question.

Sandy nodded. "I'm so sorry, Kate. But I didn't have a choice. It was her fault."

Sandy pointed at Melissa, who was on the outside of the circle trying to guide her father toward the door. When he saw Sandy point at Melissa, Mr. Harper stopped cold. He disengaged his arm from his daughter's hand and seized her by the elbow.

"How is it her fault?" the chief asked.

"It's a long story."

The chief stared at her silently like time was one thing of which he had plenty.

Sandy sighed. "Before I got the job in your store, Kate, I applied at Fabulous Fabrics."

"I thought I recognized her," Roger muttered.

"Melissa interviewed me. She said they didn't have a position at the moment, but that she would pay me double what I'd get at the store if I'd be her special assistant. She wanted me to get a job in your shop but actually be a spy for her."

"And you agreed to do that?" Kate asked coldly.

"I needed the money. And Melissa told me that spying is something all businesses do today."

"But it didn't stop at spying, did it?" the chief said in his deep voice.

"It was more than that almost from the first," Sandy admitted. She turned to Kate. "When you gave me that ad to take to the newspaper, I brought it to Melissa first and she changed it to make you look bad."

"And then you spray-painted my shop and figured the skateboarders would get the blame," Kate said.

Sandy nodded.

"And you went to Quilter's Paradise and said that I was recommending that people go to Fabulous Fabrics."

"That was Melissa's idea too, and she's the one who told me to set the fire in the dumpster."

"And was it you who followed me to the gray house?" Kate asked.

"I was supposed to spray-paint the shop again that night, but I got there just as you left and decided to follow you. Melissa wanted me to find out everything about you that I could. I slipped inside the house to see what was going on in there, but when I heard your voice I ran away. I was so scared by then that I didn't dare go back to the store."

"And why did you stop vandalizing the store after that?" Kate asked.

"Melissa told me that she'd found another way to solve the problem. She said that after Christmas she wouldn't be needing me as a spy anymore because she'd be moving to Colorado."

Kate turned to Roger. "Once Melissa figured she'd gotten you transferred, she didn't care about ruining my life any more."

Out of the corner of her eye, Kate saw Melissa's father turn red as he realized how he'd been used.

"So what about this quilt, then?" the chief asked,

clearly anxious to take charge of the questioning again.

"Late yesterday afternoon Melissa called me and said she needed me to do one last thing. I told her that I'd had enough. I was moving back to Boston and didn't want any more to do with her. That's when she told me that, if I didn't help her, she'd turn me in to the police and make it sound like the vandalism was all my fault."

"That was after she knew that you were going to quit Fabulous Fabrics rather than go with her," Kate said to Roger.

"And that one last thing she wanted you to do was this?" The chief indicated the damaged quilt.

Sandy nodded. "I still had my keys to the shop. I was going to turn them in today. So I went to the store to get a pair of shears to cut the quilt. I didn't know anyone was following me."

"Why did you drive around in that red car?" Tim asked.

"I told Melissa that I didn't want anyone to see my car near the shop at night because it might be recognized. She told me to borrow hers. Melissa made me come to the show today because she said that she wouldn't pay me until she saw with her own eyes that the quilt was ruined."

"What pathetic lies," Melissa shouted, beginning to shove her way through the crowd in Sandy's direction. One of the officers moved to block her way.

"Melissa! Is this true?" Her father's question stopped her cold.

"Oh, Daddy," she said, turning to look at him. "I

was just trying to get what I wanted. That's what you always do."

The muscles in her father's jaw bulged, but he didn't speak.

"Well," the chief said in a weary tone, "I think all those involved should take a walk with me down the street to the station so we can sort this out."

Two hours later, Kate sat on a hard bench in the front hall of the police station. She'd given her statement and promised to come back to sign it right after the holidays. Sandy, Stanford Harper, and Melissa had been in the chief's office for a long time. About twenty minutes beforehand, Harper had come out and asked Roger if he'd talk with him in another room. Roger had agreed.

Kate had left her cell phone in the car. If this went on much longer she was going to have to see if the desk sergeant would let her call her mother to tell her they would be late. The door opened. Roger and Stan Harper came out. They shook hands solemnly, and Harper went back into the chief's office. As Roger walked down the hall towards Kate he began to smile.

"What was that all about?" Kate asked.

"He wants me to come back to work for him. I told him I'd only do that if I can be permanent manager of the store here in town. No more traveling around. He agreed and gave me a big raise. I think he finally realized what I'd had to put up with from Melissa."

"Do you still want to work for him?" Kate asked.

"He's been good to me, Kate. I don't want to desert him now. Some time down the road, after you get your shop going, maybe I'll be able to start doing something more artistic again."

"What about Melissa? What's going to happen to her?"

Roger shook his head. "Stan's finally starting to understand that her problems are more serious than gifts and money can solve. He's worked out some kind of deal with the chief. I think Melissa's going to end up in a psychiatric treatment program back in Colorado."

"Is Sandy in a lot of trouble?"

"Malicious mischief. I'm not sure the chief even wants to prosecute. The worst thing she did was damage your quilt, so it depends on whether you want to push it."

"I don't. I feel sorry for Sandy. What she did was wrong, but basically she's a good but weak kid who came under the wrong person's influence." Kate smiled faintly. "I guess I'm just tenderhearted. I can even feel sorry for Melissa as long as she isn't standing right here in front of me."

Roger slipped his arm around her and held Kate close. "Let's get out of here. We have a holiday to celebrate."

Kate nodded and snuggled into his chest.

"The thing I'm most sorry about," Roger said, "is what happened to your quilt. It really was beautiful."

"It still is," Kate said. "That's our wedding quilt."

Roger looked at her questioningly.

Kate smiled. "After all, quilting is all about putting things back together. That's something I'm pretty good at. No damage has been done that can't be repaired with a row of neatly concealed stitches."

"But won't sleeping under it every night bring back bad memories?"

"After we get married—assuming of course that we do get married—there will be times when we'll get angry at each other and fight, don't you think?" Kate asked.

"Possibly," Roger said in a neutral tone.

"But at night when we get under that quilt, that row of small stitches running up the center of the quilt will remind us of what we went through to be together, and any disagreement we might have will seem minor by comparison."

"And then we can make up?" Roger asked with a grin.

Kate reached up to touch his face.

"That's the idea. That's definitely the idea."